GHOST LETTERS

BOOKS BY STEPHEN ALTER

The Phantom Isles
Ghost Letters

GHOST LETTERS

Stephen Alter

BLOOMSBURY
CHILDREN'S
BOOKS

Published by Bloomsbury U.S.A. Children's Books
175 Fifth Avenue, New York, NY 10010
Distributed to the trade by Macmillan

Library of Congress Cataloging-in-Publication Data
Alter, Stephen.
Ghost letters/Stephen Alter.—1st U.S. ed.
p. cm.
Summary: While exploring the area around his grandfather's home, Gil discovers
a bottle that carries messages into the past, finds a genie in a letter, and three letters
that were never delivered but would have changed the course of history.
ISBN-13: 978-1-58234-739-4 · ISBN-10: 1-58234-739-5 (hardcover)
[1. Space and time—Fiction. 2. Letters—Fiction. 3. Genies—Fiction.
4. Grandfathers—Fiction.] I. Title.
PZ7.A46373Gh 2008   [Fic]—dc22   2007030844

First U.S. Edition 2008
Typeset by Westchester Book Composition
Printed in the U.S.A. by Quebecor World Fairfield
2   4   6   8   10   9   7   5   3   1

For Rohan and Suresh

My letters! all dead paper, mute and white!
And yet they seem alive and quivering
Against my tremulous hands . . .

ELIZABETH BARRETT BROWNING

If all the world were paper,
And all the seas were ink . . .

ANONYMOUS, 1641

GHOST LETTERS

Stooped under the weight of a bulging mailbag, the ancient postman trudges along his route. The frayed brim of a gray blue hat is pulled low over his eyes. He plods silently down the street, turning off where the old cart road used to run from Boston to Hornswoggle Bay, now a quiet cul-de-sac lined with a dozen homes. Years ago, there were farms along this route, but the land has been consumed by sprawling suburbs. At places the old stone walls can still be seen, though the furrowed fields have been covered over by lawns and plantings of juniper and rhododendron, as well as the occasional swimming pool. Where barns and silos once stood are rows upon rows of anonymous dwellings. The postman ignores these modern homes.

In the gray twilight, he is a ghostly apparition passing across driveways, through hedges and over sidewalks, between piles of freshly raked leaves, retracing the invisible alignment of the cart road that has long since disappeared. Children playing street hockey do not notice him. A dog looks up, ear cocked, but doesn't bark. The postman carries on, as if the suburbs had never been built. He crosses the backyards of split-level homes, once a cow pasture, now divided into half-acre lots. New mailboxes line the street, but he doesn't stop.

Slouched with age, a figure vaporous as smoke, the postman travels through a different era, a simpler, less cluttered age, when a first-class stamp cost five cents and the letter carrier knew everyone along his route by name. Now he is invisible, a figure lost in time, an unknown postman from the past . . .

1
Gripe Water

The trail was clearly marked, even as it twisted down the hill, through an overgrown tangle of scrubby pines and stunted maples. Gil wasn't sure exactly where he was headed, though the sign a quarter mile back read RATTLE BEACH, with an arrow pointing in this direction. He still couldn't see the ocean, and when he finally came out of the trees, there was a dense patch of thorns and fireweed. Another hundred yards farther on he came to a broad shelf of granite that overlooked the gray Atlantic. Fifty feet below him, down a natural staircase in the rocks, lay a ragged crescent of pebbles and shingle, littered with tin cans and other flotsam. It wasn't like any beach Gil had ever seen before—no sand at all. The water was much too rough and cold for swimming this time of year.

Gil kicked a stone in disappointment and disgust. The grubby fingernail of beach only added to his unhappiness. After being expelled from McCauley Prep School a week ago, he had come to stay with his grandfather, who lived in an old stone house up the hill. It was bad enough to leave his friends behind and listen to his parents scolding and complaining about his future being destroyed. But worse than that was ending up here in a dead-end town called Carville, on the southern shore of Massachusetts. He liked his grandfather, who was a sort-of-famous poet, but there was only so much they could talk about. After a game of Scrabble last night, Gil had pretended he was sleepy and gone to bed, lying awake and trying to figure out how he was going to survive the next few weeks. There wasn't even a TV in the house, or a computer. It was like living in a museum. The only thing he could do was walk the dog and read old magazines whose subscriptions had run out long before he was born.

Getting thrown out of school was kind of like being on vacation, except everyone else was in class. Though Gil didn't mind taking a break from homework, math problems and pop quizzes, he felt a bit like a castaway. He had never been very good at making friends, but this year he had met a couple of classmates at McCauley Prep with whom he liked to hang out. Now he was alone again, standing on a deserted beach with nothing to do, as bored as a bear in a zoo. He picked up one of the flat stones and tried to skip it across the water, but the waves were too rough. About a hundred yards from shore he could see a couple of lobster buoys. A motorboat went past, but there was no other sign of life, except for the gulls that wheeled overhead. Gil kicked at a soda can half buried in the beach. There was also a frayed length of rope, and slimy fingers of kelp wrapped around a piece of Styrofoam that looked as if

4

it had been chewed by a shark. Broken clamshells lay among the stones and scattered bits of a crab that one of the gulls must have eaten for breakfast.

As Gil turned around to head back up the rocks, he saw something blue floating at the edge of the water. It was an old bottle. A wave rolled in and he heard the grating sound of pebbles rattled by the tide. Reaching down, Gil fished the bottle out. Though covered with sea scum, it was a dazzling blue—almost purple. He rinsed it off when the next wave came in, and held it up to the sun. The glass was scuffed with sand and the base was chipped, but otherwise it was intact. There wasn't anything inside, as far as Gil could see, but the bottle was sealed with a cork that looked as if it hadn't been opened for years.

Molded into the glass on the front of the bottle were a few lines of raised letters—some kind of brand name. But these were badly worn and hard to read. Tilting the bottle to one side, Gil deciphered the words:

A. K. Jaddoowalla's
Finest Indian
GRIPE WATER

Gil didn't know what it meant, but he suddenly had an idea. Rummaging in the pocket of his jacket, he found a pencil stub and a scrap of paper he'd been carrying around for more than a month. It was an old notice for an overdue book from the McCauley Library.

Putting the bottle down, Gil flattened the paper on one of the rocks and scribbled a message:

Help! I'm stranded on a desert island. Save me!
Gil Mendelson-Finch

He felt a little foolish when he folded the paper, yet couldn't help but smile to himself. With some tugging, he was able to uncork the bottle. It was dry inside, and as he stuffed the paper down the neck, Gil wondered if anyone would ever find his message. Of course, they'd know it was a joke, but somehow, writing those words made him feel better.

Replacing the cork, he threw the bottle out into the waves, as far as he could. Then he watched its blue shape bobbing on the surface for a while. By the time he climbed back up the rocks and glanced over his shoulder, the bottle had disappeared.

2
The Calligrapher's Apprentice

More than a hundred years earlier and half a world away, in one of the narrow lanes that run from Ajeebgarh Railway Station, through the spice bazaar, to the Central Post and Telegraph Office, stands a small shop with a canvas awning and a sign in English, Urdu and Hindi.

Ghulam Rusool
Letter Writer & Calligrapher
Government Forms, Petitions,
General Correspondence & Poetry

The shop has a low, wooden desk and cushions for the letter writer and his clients to sit upon. Most of the people who come to Ghulam Rusool are illiterate—villagers from the hills, laborers on the tea estates or indigo plantations, and other townspeople who never learned to read or write. As each of them dictates letters and applications, judicial documents and messages of congratulation or complaint, the letter writer carefully transcribes their words in any of seven languages he knows.

At the back of the shop, his apprentice, Sikander, prepares and mixes the ink.

It's not an easy job. Every day, after his lessons finish at the madrassa behind the mosque, Sikander hurries to the letter writer's shop and settles down to work. There are dozens of different kinds of ink: blue, red and green, but mostly varying shades of black. Though ignorant people think there is only one color of black, Sikander can name eight different tints—from the feathers of a crow to the dark night of the moon.

For ordinary ink, Sikander uses soot gathered from lamps in the town. Each morning, before going to school, he does his rounds of the neighborhood, collecting the oily black residue wiped off glass chimneys. The soot that he collects is mixed with water and shellac from the gum trees that grow in the foothills above Ajeebgarh. Their trunks and branches are nicked hundreds of times, and the resin that oozes out of the trees gives the India ink its permanence and a polished sheen. The letter writer uses this for most of the documents he prepares, but there are special recipes for other inks that have their own unusual purposes.

The calligrapher is an old man, with a white beard and stooped shoulders, but he still has a steady hand. He shares secrets of the craft with his apprentice, whispering the mysteries of the written word. One kind of ink is always used for correspondence between two lovers—the charred bark of an ashoka tree mixed with the attar of roses. Another is employed to write a curse—the darkest black of all, made from the burned remains of funerary flowers mixed with the glue of donkey's hooves. There's an ink for writing an old man's will, which uses indelible pigments squeezed from a mountain cherry and the singed wings of moths burned by a candle flame. Yet another ink requires venom from a scorpion's tail, and is prepared only for signing a death warrant by the king. But the most magical ink of all is used for writing couplets to summon a djinn. Never before has the calligrapher revealed the mysteries of this ink, which traces verses that conceal forbidden secrets. Three different kinds of residue are mixed together: the carbonized seeds of a custard apple, the ashes from a water pipe smoked by a wandering dervish and the soot from a genie's lamp.

Sikander holds his breath as he grinds the blend of ingredients with a mortar and pestle until it is as fine as gunpowder. Then with trembling hands, he stirs in a measure of gooseberry wine. When the ink is the right consistency, a shade of black he has never seen before, Sikander shows it to the calligrapher. The old man sniffs the mixture cautiously. He nods approval and asks for his pen—the one with the nib made of gold and a stem of the clearest jade.

3
Trash Hill

Gil let Kipling off his leash as soon as they crossed the street into the town forest. The old dog put his nose to the ground and headed straight for the trees. A scruffy mix of English setter and bloodhound, Kipling was fourteen years old, the same age as Gil. Though the dog was completely deaf and almost blind, he had a nose that could find anything from a half-eaten tuna sandwich to a chipmunk hiding in a brush pile.

It was about three in the afternoon and there was nobody else in the park, except for a dozen geese near the old ice pond. The birds raised their necks and gawked at Kipling as he raced off across the uncut grass.

Gil whistled for the dog, though he knew it wouldn't do any good. Kipling had a habit of searching out anything that smelled bad and rolling in it. A few days back, he had discovered a rotten blue jay's egg that must have fallen out of its nest. Throwing himself upon the cracked white shell, he had writhed about with dogged pleasure, grunting in delight and covering himself with its stench, as if it were the sweetest perfume. Bits of greenish yolk and eggshell clung to the fur around his neck. Walking Kipling back home, Gil almost threw up, it stank so bad. Worse than skunk. He and his grandfather had to hose the dog off in the backyard, then shampoo him twice before they could let him back in the house. Even then, the faint odor of rotten egg lingered on his fur.

After that, Gil had decided to keep Kipling on a leash whenever they went out for a walk. But today he'd given in and unclipped him, knowing how much the dog liked to run free. Now he wished he hadn't.

"Kip!" he shouted, chasing the dog. "Hey, Kip! Come back here, boy . . . Kipling, you stupid mutt!"

Gil knew there wasn't any point in calling. Kipling couldn't hear him from even three feet away, and by now he was a hundred yards ahead, a shaggy brown torpedo with a ragged tail. Maybe he'd caught the scent of a deer, or a coyote. Gil wrapped the leash around his fist as he ran, cursing the dog under his breath.

As he reached the edge of the woods, dead leaves crackled under his shoes. Pushing aside branches, he tried to spot Kipling in the underbrush. There was no sign of the dog.

"Kip!" he shouted again, more out of frustration than from any hope of being heard.

A moment later Gil heard a bark. It wasn't the gruff baying noise that Kipling usually made, but higher pitched, an exclamation of alarm. Hurrying in the direction of the sound, Gil had to climb over a fallen oak and wade through blueberry bushes. He hoped there wasn't any poison ivy. Where the trees ended stood a rusty, chain-link fence with a large sign.

DANGER
NO ENTRY
CARVILLE TOWN DUMP
POLICE TAKE NOTICE

Beyond the fence lay a marshy area full of swamp grass and ferns. Fifty yards farther on rose a humpbacked hill overgrown with vines and weeds. Gil could see Kipling sniffing about near the foot of the hill. He tried calling again but knew it was pointless. Moving along the fence to his left, he found a place where the wires had been torn open, a hole just large enough to scramble through. Glancing back at the sign with hesitation, Gil got down on his hands and knees and crawled inside.

By this time Kipling had stopped barking. Because of the marsh, Gil circled around until he found a section that wasn't as muddy as the rest, though his shoes squelched as he jumped across. When Gil reached the dog, Kipling was standing still, one forepaw raised. Even though he wasn't a trained hunting dog, his nose and tail pointed straight out, quivering with excitement. Coming up beside him, Gil clipped the leash to his collar.

"Come on," he said. "Crazy pooch!"

But Kipling wouldn't move. He gave another bark and Gil looked up to see what the dog was pointing at. By this time, he had realized the hill was actually a garbage heap, a huge mountain of rubble and discarded junk. It looked as if it had been years since anyone had dumped things there, and most of the mound was covered in creepers. Bushes were growing out of old tires, and a stunted birch tree had taken root in a cracked bathtub half filled with dirt. One corner of a rusting refrigerator jutted out from under an avalanche of rotting leaves and dead branches. There was even an old sofa half buried in the hill, moss growing on the cushions. Kipling was pointing to the left of this, at a dented tin mailbox with a red plastic flag. It was attached to an iron stand and leaned precariously to one side, sticking out of the junk pile.

Gil couldn't understand why Kipling was pointing at the rusty old mailbox. Maybe a raccoon had its burrow in the hill. Tugging impatiently at the leash, Gil was startled to hear a voice behind him.

"Does your dog bite?"

Swiveling around, Gil saw a girl about his age, sitting astride a mountain bike. She had black windblown hair and dark brown skin. The sleeves on her sweatshirt were rolled up to her elbows, and the knees on her jeans were torn. She had one foot on the ground and the other rested on a pedal. The wheels and sprockets of the bike were covered in mud.

"I heard him barking," the girl said. "What's his name?"

"Kipling," said Gil. "Don't worry, he doesn't bite."

"Do you live nearby?" the girl asked.

Gil nodded, eyeing her cautiously. "I just moved here last week."

"I'm Nargis," she said.

"Hi. My name's Gil," he said, winding Kip's leash around his hand self-consciously.

"How did you get in here?" Nargis asked. She had a blunt way of speaking but seemed friendly enough.

"There's a hole in the fence," he said, wondering how she had entered the dump. "I guess we're not supposed to be inside this place."

"Well . . . ," said Nargis. "There really isn't anybody to stop you. The dump has been closed for years. There's a new recycling center and mulching station on the other side, over there beyond the trees."

"Must be a whole lot of junk buried here," Gil said.

"Yeah. I call it Trash Hill. If you climb to the top, you can see the ocean."

Kipling let out an impatient whimper.

"Why's he pointing at that mailbox?" said Nargis. "Do you think there's something inside?"

"Maybe." Gil shrugged. "He sure smells something."

"Why don't we take a look?" Nargis suggested.

She lowered her bike to the ground and stepped over the handlebars. Climbing up the side of the hill, Nargis opened the mailbox to peer inside. Almost immediately, she recoiled, wrinkling her nose.

"Gross! That's totally disgusting . . ." Nargis made a face. "It stinks . . . Take a look!"

Gil wasn't sure he wanted to find out what was inside the mailbox, though he climbed up beside Nargis and leaned over to see what it contained. The stench was both sweet and rotten at the same time, like a combination of lilacs and rancid cheese, an odor of perfumed decay. But worse than that was the source of the smell—a skeleton's hand, cut off at the wrist.

"Whoa!" said Gil, stumbling back in horror. "Omigod, that's sick! Let's get out of here!"

4
Versification

In the Name of the Empress of India, make way,
O Lords of the Jungle, wherever you roam,
The woods are awake at the end of the day—
We exiles are waiting for letters from Home.
Let the robber retreat, and the tiger turn tail—
In the Name of the Empress, the Overland Mail!

"Doggerel," muttered Prescott Finch to himself as he set aside a well-thumbed copy of Rudyard Kipling's verses, "but poetry nonetheless."

He turned back to the half-written stanzas scrolling out of his Remington. Prescott had used the same typewriter for forty-five years—an ancient portable, with a battered case. Everyone else was using computers now, but he still composed his poems on a typewriter. Lifting the paper, he read over what he had just written:

A letter goes undelivered,
Words written but unread.
We always blame the postman…
By air, by sea, by snail

"Let the robber retreat, and the tiger turn tail— / In the Name of the Empress, the Overland Mail!" Prescott recited under his breath. Kipling's rhyme and rhythm stuck to his mind like chewing gum on the seat of your pants.

The postman knows his route
Names, numbers and address

His own words didn't sound right, even as a first draft. Impatiently, Prescott stripped the half-written page from the typewriter, crumpled it into a ball, then fed another sheet into the roller, lining it up carefully.

He started again:

Trudging out of history, one slow stride at a time,
He shoulders a mailbag full of letters unreceived,
Lost missives, postcards gone astray, an errant rhyme.
Sore of foot, numb-kneed, the postman seems aggrieved.

Outside his office window, Prescott could see afternoon sunlight filtering through the last yellow leaves on the hickory tree at the edge of the lawn. Farther off, in the distance, lay the warped surface of the Atlantic reaching toward a clouded horizon. Prescott's eyes drifted up the curtains and across the wall to a black-and-white photograph in an oval frame. It was a portrait of an elderly woman. She had gray hair pulled back in a bun and wore a black dress over a high-collared lace blouse. Though her features were sad and wrinkled, there was a melancholy beauty about her, and her eyes seemed to be searching for something, or someone, beyond the camera.

Just then, the kitchen door banged and Prescott heard footsteps running through the house. His fingers were still touching the Remington's keys when Gil burst through the office door with Kipling on his leash.

"Grandpa!" Gil could barely talk, after running all the way. "Grandpa. We found something . . ."

"What?" said Prescott.

"There's an old mailbox in the town dump . . . Kipling found it . . . When we opened the mailbox, there was a skeleton's hand inside."

Gasping for breath, Gil leaned down and pressed his stomach to get rid of a stitch in his side.

"Hold on," said Prescott, rising from his chair. "Easy now!"

In his excitement, the dog had wrapped the leash around Prescott's leg. While getting himself untangled, he noticed a girl standing awkwardly in the doorway.

"This is Nargis," said Gil. "She lives down the street. We both saw the hand . . ."

Prescott nodded in Nargis's direction, then asked, "Are you sure it's a skeleton?"

"Yeah," said Gil. "I think we should call the police."

"Slow down a moment," said Prescott. "It's not some kind of practical joke, is it?"

"No way. It's real," said Gil.

Nargis added, "Just the bones of the hand with no arm attached. And it smells really bad."

5
A Moving Finger

Sikander is surprised to see the calligrapher writing in English. Most of the poems Ghulam Rusool transcribes are written in Farsi or Urdu, with the script flowing from right to left. Today, however, the calligrapher pens the verses from left to right. Edging closer, Sikander peers over the old man's shoulder, curious to see what he is writing with the magical ink. Urdu is Sikander's mother tongue, but he has taught himself English with the calligrapher's help. He also has a friend named Lawrence, the son of a tea planter, with whom he speaks English. Sikander scans the verses on the page as each word emerges from Ghulam Rusool's pen.

Awake! For Morning in the bowl of Night
Has flung the Stone that puts the Stars to Flight:
And Lo! The Hunter of the East has caught
The Sultan's turret in a Noose of Light . . .

The moving finger writes; and, having writ,
Moves on: nor all thy Piety nor Wit
Shall lure it back to cancel half a Line,
Nor all thy Tears wash out a Word of it . . .

When the calligrapher finishes writing these stanzas from the *Rubaiyat of Omar Khayyam*, he takes a green glass jar full of sand and dusts it on the page to blot the ink, shaking it slightly. Pouring the sand back into the jar, he chooses a blank envelope from his writing desk and addresses it with ordinary ink. Ghulam Rusool folds the single sheet of verses and slips it into the envelope. After gluing the flap shut, he seals it with red wax, melted over a candle flame. Using his signet ring, the calligrapher leaves the impression of an eight-pointed star.

Once all of this is done, he hands the envelope to Sikander, along with a silver four-anna coin, and tells him to run to the post office and mail the letter immediately. Hurrying down the lane, the boy feels an important urgency, knowing the letter contains a vital message for someone far away. He often posts letters for Ghulam Rusool's clients, but today there seems to be a greater purpose in his step as he dodges through the crowded lane, pushing past fruit vendors and donkeys, loiterers and women shopping for spices.

The Central Post and Telegraph Office has always been a mysterious and marvelous place for Sikander, with high arched ceilings and a counter that he can barely reach. It seems as if the post office is a link with the world outside of Ajeebgarh, places

Sikander can only dream of visiting. China. Persia. Africa. Europe. America. Behind the polished brass grille sits a clerk with spectacles balanced on the end of his nose. As Sikander hands the letter over to him, the clerk glances at the clock on the wall.

"Twenty-two minutes past four," he says with a smile. "You got here just in time . . . Eight minutes to spare."

"And what if I'd been late?" asks Sikander with a grin.

"I would have told you to come back tomorrow."

"No, sir. This letter must go today."

"And it will," says the clerk, putting the envelope on the scale and raising his eyebrows. "A first-class letter to Cairo . . . Two ounces . . . Four annas."

Sikander hands over the coin and the clerk takes a pair of two-anna stamps from his drawer, both with pictures of the maharajah of Ajeebgarh, and affixes them to the envelope. Then with a decisive gesture, he thumps the ink pad and the envelope to cancel the postage.

"How long will it take to reach Cairo?" asks Sikander.

"Let's see . . . At six o'clock tomorrow morning it will travel by train on the *Himalayan Mail*. After thirty-six hours, the letter will reach Bombay and be put on a ship to Suez. A couple weeks' voyage . . . Then from there, I suppose it goes by camel to Cairo. Three weeks altogether . . . four at the most."

Thanking the postal clerk, Sikander stares up at the high ceiling and imagines himself riding the train from Ajeebgarh to Bombay, then boarding the ship and sailing across the Arabian Sea, and finally climbing onto a camel to travel over the sand dunes to Cairo.

As he leaves the Post and Telegraph Office, Sikander decides to take a shortcut home. Crossing the railway bridge over the Magor River, which flows through Ajeebgarh, he climbs down the steps to the water, where washermen are pounding laundry on the rocks. Continuing along the riverbank, Sikander passes a couple of boats tied up near the shore. The Magor is a dark green color with a sluggish current that drifts between muddy banks where buffaloes wallow in the backwaters. A few miles below Ajeebgarh, the Magor joins a much swifter river called the Arun that eventually runs into the Ganga. From there the water pours out into the Bay of Bengal. Sikander has often dreamed of climbing into one of the boats, cutting the ropes free, and drifting from one river to the next, until he reaches the sea.

He stops to watch a white-necked stork standing in the shallows of the river, its long beak ready to snap up a fish. Just then, Sikander catches sight of something blue at the water's edge. Going closer, he sees a bottle sealed with a cork. To reach it, he has to wade into the river, and the stork flies off. Picking up the bright blue bottle, Sikander finds it is empty, except for a scrap of paper rolled up inside.

6

The Yankee Mahal

Leaving Kipling at home this time, Gil and Nargis climbed into Prescott's car—a battered Volkswagen that rattled and shook. Instead of crossing the park and scrambling through the fence, they drove around to the other side of the town dump, and parked next to the recycling center and mulching station. There didn't seem to be anyone else around. Nargis led them through the gate and down a dirt track to Trash Hill. Prescott had brought his walking stick, but he didn't really use it, except to poke a hole in the rusty remains of the old refrigerator as Gil and Nargis nervously approached the mailbox.

"There it is," said Gil.

"A perfect place for junk mail," Prescott joked. He didn't seem convinced about the skeletal hand.

Nargis asked, "Who's going to open it?"

"Go ahead," said Gil.

"Why don't you?" she said with a nervous smile.

Gil looked across at his grandfather, who nodded encouragingly. Reaching out his hand, which was shaking badly, Gil flipped the mailbox open. For a moment nobody moved. Then Nargis leaned down and squinted. There wasn't any smell.

"It's empty," said Gil.

"That's impossible." Nargis echoed his surprise.

"But the hand was here just half an hour ago. I swear we saw it," said Gil, staring into the empty mailbox, then looking back at Prescott. "Grandpa, you have to believe me. It was a skeleton's hand. The bones were a yellowish white and it smelled awful."

"It's true," said Nargis. "It was really gross!"

Prescott nodded and shrugged, a skeptical frown adding to the wrinkles on his face.

"Sure," he said. "Maybe so."

+   +   +

When he had first arrived in Carville, a week ago, the last thing Gil expected was to have anything unusual happen. Staying in a musty old house overlooking the sea wasn't exactly the choice he would have made for himself. But nobody seemed interested in his opinion, particularly since he'd just been expelled from school. Both his parents traveled all the time for work, and there was nobody to stay with him at home in Connecticut. This was the main reason Gil had been put in boarding school in the first place. Two days after he was thrown out of McCauley Prep, his mother had to leave on a business trip, and his father had driven him up to Prescott's house.

As their car pulled into the driveway, Kipling had barked at them but came up wagging his tail and sniffed Gil's hand. Prescott greeted his son-in-law with an awkward handshake. The two men had never seen eye to eye. When Prescott invited them inside, Gil's father thanked him but said he needed to get back to New York to catch a flight. Warning his son to "behave yourself and make up for what you've done," Gil's father drove off.

"He's a busy man, your dad . . . ," said Prescott, tugging at his moustache to hide his disapproval.

Gil looked at the old man with an uncertain smile. Prescott was close to seventy, but his shoulders carried his age lightly. He picked up one of Gil's bags and led him to his room at the far end of the house, up a flight of stone stairs. The bedroom was a large, gloomy space with a tilted wardrobe and bookcases filled with murder mysteries. The one window looked out into the woods.

Setting the suitcase at the foot of the bed, Prescott put a reassuring arm around his grandson's shoulder.

"Don't worry," he said in an understanding voice. "Your mother probably never told you this, but I was kicked out of McCauley too. It isn't the end of the world."

Gil glanced up with surprise. "Why were you thrown out of school?" he asked.

"We'll talk about that later," said his grandfather. "Now, I imagine you're thirsty. How about some tea?"

Gil had been to the house a couple of times before. It always reminded him of a medieval castle with heavy stone archways and turrets supporting a slate roof. After passing through several doorways, down a long hall, they came out into the kitchen, which was much brighter than the rest of the house. On the counter was a plate of cookies.

Gil sat down as his grandfather opened the refrigerator and took out a jug of tea. Filling two glasses with ice he poured the amber liquid over the cubes. Though he hated tea, Gil didn't want to say anything to Prescott, who squeezed a wedge of lemon into each glass.

"Two spoons of sugar or three?" his grandfather asked.

"Just one, thanks," said Gil, hoping he wouldn't gag.

"Here you go," Prescott said. "Have a cookie."

Still dazed from his journey and the dizzying ride up the coast, Gil felt a little sick to his stomach. But when he took a cookie and tasted it, he realized that he was hungry. The gingery sweetness crumbled on his tongue, and it was gone before he knew it. After this he helped himself to another, which went down just as quickly.

Kipling edged closer to the kitchen counter, his nose snorting expectantly and his mouth slobbering. Prescott gave him a cookie from the plate, then told him to get lost. Gil's tea sat untouched until the ice cubes had almost melted. Raising the glass at last, he sniffed the fragrance, surprised at how different it was from the soapy, dishwater smell of the tea his mother made at home. Cautiously, he tried a sip and the flavor startled him. It actually tasted good. Gil closed his eyes and took a large swallow.

"Darjeeling. Orange pekoe. First flush," his grandfather

said. "Made with rainwater so it doesn't ruin the taste. You know this house was built with tea and ice."

"What do you mean?" said Gil.

"My great-granduncle—your great-great-great-granduncle—Ezekiel Finch made his fortune as a Yankee trader, shipping tea from India to America," said Prescott. "He also used to ship ice from America to India."

Gil gave his grandfather a skeptical glance.

"It's true. The ice came from the pond on the other side of the hill. This was long before there were refrigerators. During winter, Ezekiel hired teams of men to cut the frozen surface of the pond into rectangular blocks, which they hauled down to the harbor on horse-drawn sleighs. The ice was covered with sawdust for insulation, and loaded into the holds of clipper ships. Half of it melted by the time they reached India, but the ice could still be sold to English colonials living there, so they could have cold drinks in summer."

Gil took another sip from his glass and listened intently as Prescott continued.

"The cargo of tea that Ezekiel brought back from India weighed much less than ice, so his ships needed ballast. Most sea captains filled the holds of their clippers with rocks to keep them on an even keel. When they returned to New England, the ballast stones were thrown into the harbor or onto shore. All along the coast of Massachusetts you'll find rocks from India, China and other countries around the world. Instead of discarding the ballast stones, Ezekiel decided to store them.

Once he had enough, he built this house and called it the Yankee Mahal. But Ezekiel never really lived in this house. Soon after it was constructed in 1840, he sailed for India and never came back."

"Why did he do that?" asked Gil.

"Nobody's really sure, but the story is he fell in love with a woman who rejected him. Ezekiel went away brokenhearted to a lonely exile in the East. Our ancestor was a colorful character. Everyone's heard of Paul Revere and his midnight ride," said Prescott, "but not many people know that Ezekiel Finch delivered an equally important message to the people of Boston."

"What kind of message?" said Gil.

"It was during the War of 1812. In those days, Carville was still known as Hornswoggle Bay, and a British navy frigate sailed in to blockade the harbor. Ezekiel Finch was only ten years old at the time. His father was the harbormaster, and he wrote a letter to the governor, warning him that the British were coming. Ezekiel didn't have a horse, but his family owned a mule named Sally. Taking the letter and jumping onto Sally's back, Ezekiel rode all the way to Boston in less than three hours. The letter he carried is preserved by the Carville Historical Society. They also have one of Sally's horseshoes on display."

"Why isn't he famous like Paul Revere?" said Gil.

Prescott shrugged. "I guess it's just the way history gets recorded. Some things are remembered and others are forgotten. Paul Revere probably wouldn't be as famous today if Henry

Wadsworth Longfellow hadn't written a poem about him. You remember how it goes:

> *"Listen my children and you shall hear,*
> *Of the midnight ride of Paul Revere . . ."*

Gil nodded. "We were supposed to read it in school, but it was kind of long and boring."

"Well, at least you didn't have to memorize the whole thing," said Prescott. "When I was in seventh grade, we had to recite it for a school assembly."

"Maybe you should write a poem about Ezekiel Finch," said Gil. "That way people will remember him."

"Not a bad idea," said Prescott thoughtfully.

"I guess you'd have to find lots of words that rhyme with *Finch*," said Gil, "and *Sally*."

"That's the easy part," said Prescott. "Do you want to see a picture of your ancestor?"

Before Gil could reply, his grandfather got to his feet and headed out of the kitchen. There was a formal parlor downstairs that was almost never used. It was a gloomy, dusty room with heavy curtains on the windows. When Prescott turned on the lights, Gil could see that the furniture was shrouded in dustcovers, and there was a musty smell of old wood and fabric. On the wall opposite the fireplace hung a large oil painting in an ornate frame. It was a picture of a boy on a gray mule, riding through farmland. The boy was dressed in blue breeches, with a loose shirt blowing in the wind. When Gil looked at the picture more closely, he could see that Ezekiel was holding a letter in one hand.

"Sally was used for plowing fields," said Prescott. "She wasn't meant to be ridden, certainly not thirty miles to Boston."

Gil tried to imagine what it would be like to ride bareback all that way; it made him feel sore just thinking about it. On the other side of the room was a later portrait of Ezekiel Finch, painted just before he left for India. There was a resemblance to the boy in the other picture. His eyes were the same pale blue, and his mouth was similar—neither a smile nor a frown. His hair had receded and he was wearing a formal black frock coat, with a red silk scarf knotted at his throat. On a table in the painting, next to Ezekiel's right hand, lay a jeweled inkstand set with rubies and emeralds. A quill pen rested beside it. Prescott pointed to the inkstand.

"That's a gift Ezekiel was going to give Camellia Stubbs, the woman he loved. Ezekiel knew that Camellia had a passion for writing and he ordered it especially for her, all the way from India. The stand was made of gold, encrusted with jewels, and the two ink bottles were the finest crystal. Supposedly, it cost eight hundred dollars in those days. Of course, when Camellia turned down his proposal, Ezekiel was heartbroken. Nobody knows what happened to the inkstand. There's a rumor he buried it before he sailed for India, but it's never been found."

"If it cost eight hundred dollars back then, it must be worth a ton of money now," said Gil, peering at the painting.

7

Curried Okra

By the time Nargis got home, her mother was already cooking dinner. The smell of frying onions and the peppery tang of spices greeted her before she opened the front door. Though Nargis loved the food her mother made, she was self-conscious about the smells of Indian cooking that drifted out of their house into the neighborhood. Most of the other people on their street had backyard barbecues, and the charred odor of grilled meat filled the air. Nargis's family were vegetarians, and the cooking smells from their home were mostly frying onions, ginger and garlic, mixed with cumin and coriander.

"Come and help me," Savita Khanna said as Nargis entered the kitchen.

"I've got homework, Mom!" said Nargis, though she knew the excuse wouldn't work.

"Then why were you cycling around, when you should have been studying instead?" her mother asked.

Catching sight of a pile of okra on the kitchen counter, Nargis was glad to see that her mother was cooking her favorite vegetable. She was still unsettled by what had happened at Trash Hill—discovering the skeletal hand, then having it disappear. The whole thing just didn't make sense. Nargis had decided not to say anything about what she'd seen. She knew her parents didn't like her bicycling alone around the town dump.

"Wash your hands," said her mother. "Then you can cut the bhindi for me."

Though Nargis was born in Carville and had lived here all her life, her parents had emigrated to the United States from India, almost twenty years ago.

"Mom, why can't you call it okra instead of bhindi?" said Nargis as she rinsed her hands in the sink. The dark green vegetables were about three inches long, a tapered pod with ridges on the sides and a furry skin.

"A bhindi is a bhindi," her mother said patiently as she peeled ginger and garlic.

"But it's also okra," said Nargis. Picking up a knife, she cut off the end of one of the pods. It was sticky and clung to the blade. Inside, she could see the glutinous white seeds. Raw okra didn't look very appetizing, but when it was fried up with onions and spices, there wasn't anything Nargis liked better. She was already starving.

"You can call it what you want, but hurry and finish cutting—quickly now," her mother said. After Nargis had chopped most of the bhindi into segments, her mother added, "You know, some people also call it 'lady fingers.'"

Looking down at the vegetables, Nargis shuddered. "That's disgusting," she said.

As she sliced the last few bhindi, she remembered the bare bones and knuckles in the mailbox and the flowery stench. Imagining five green fingers on a dead woman's hand, Nargis almost dropped the knife. Suddenly her appetite was gone.

"By the way, there was a letter for you," her mother said. "It's on the table in the hall, next to the phone."

Nargis was puzzled. She had no idea who would be writing to her. Most of her friends sent e-mails or instant messages. After wiping her hands, she picked up the letter and took it to her room.

Tearing the envelope open, Nargis took out the letter. It had been photocopied; only her name was written by hand in blue ink.

Dear *Nargis* :

This is a chain letter that was started in 1936 and hasn't been broken since. Within three days you must make six copies of this letter and send it to the names and addresses below. Remove the first name from the list and add your name and address at the bottom. It's very important that you mail this letter within three days. Make sure you also copy the poem below:

Send off this letter and join the chain,
Words linked together for better or worse,
Pass on good luck, again and again,
But if you break this chain, beware the curse!

By sending this letter on, you will bring yourself good luck. The day after she mailed this letter, Tillie Markham of Elkhart, Indiana, won $100,000 in the state lottery. Ebenezer Cole, of Sheffield, England, had been suffering from arthritis for ten years and could barely stand up. Soon after mailing this letter, he was able to walk five miles without a cane.

Warning: If you don't send this letter, it could bring bad luck. Melody Service of Portland, Oregon, forgot to send it and after the third day, she lost her job. Even worse, Xavier Salinas of San Juan, Puerto Rico, failed to send the letter and had a fatal heart attack. Don't forget to copy and mail this letter immediately.

Sincerely yours,
Rachel Reichel

"That's so dumb!" said Nargis out loud. "Who would ever believe something like this?"

Rachel Reichel was a girl who had been in her class in third grade. She had moved from Carville to St. Louis and Nargis hadn't heard from her again, until now. It annoyed her to think that anyone would be superstitious enough to send on a chain letter. She certainly didn't believe it brought good luck or bad. Nargis had got several messages like this as e-mails, and whenever they appeared on the screen, she always hit the delete button. Tearing the letter into pieces, she tossed it into the wastebasket.

8
A Bottled Message

As Sikander hurries through the maze of streets that lead to his house in the heart of Ajeebgarh, the sun has turned a buttery gold and is already melting into the horizon. Hearing the call to prayer, he dashes into his room and hides the blue bottle under the pillow on his bed, then runs to join his father at the neighborhood mosque.

After their evening prayers, Sikander walks back home with his father, who is one of the maharajah's royal bodyguards. Mehboob Khan has a thick black beard, parted in the middle. He wears a khaki uniform and a green turban with a flared coxcomb. There are rumors in the town that British troops are advancing on Ajeebgarh and threatening to attack. When Sikander nervously asks his father if this is true, Mehboob Khan nods.

"Is there really going to be a war?" Sikander asks.

"Unlikely," his father says. "It's a political game. But you never know where that might lead."

"Why are the British sending their army?" asks Sikander.

His father laughs as they reach their home. "Because of a four-anna stamp."

Sikander is puzzled by his father's answer but afraid to ask any more. Instead of going indoors, the two of them climb to the roof of the house. The sky is darkening as father and son open the pigeon coop and begin to feed their pet birds. These pigeons are bred for competitions and trained to carry messages. Some are already perched and waiting while others come circling home, tumbling out of the air with a flurry of wings. Calling to the birds in a gentle murmur, Sikander's father holds out a handful of millet seeds and the birds descend upon him. Four pigeons settle on Sikander's arm, another on his shoulder and one on his head. As he feeds them, they coo and gurgle with excitement.

Only after the birds have been fed is Sikander able to steal away for a few minutes and retrieve the bottle. As much as anything, the color intrigues him. It is a deep blue, almost the same tint as the stones of lapis lazuli in his mother's favorite necklace. Held up to the lamplight, the glass seems to glow. Though Sikander removes the cork without difficulty, he has trouble taking out the paper, which sticks in the neck of the bottle. Finally, after shaking it hard, the scrolled message falls into his lap. Sikander unrolls it slowly and reads the words:

Help! I'm stranded on a desert island. Save me!
Gil Mendelson-Finch

Turning the paper over, he sees something printed on the other side:

McCauley Preparatory School
Library Overdue Notice
October 6, 2007
Dickens, Charles *Great Expectations*
Checked out by Gil Mendelson-Finch 9/6/2007
If this book isn't returned immediately you will be
charged 25 cents per day.

Before he can figure out what it means, Sikander hears his mother calling him for dinner. Hurriedly, he corks the bottle and hides it under his pillow again, along with the scribbled note.

◆　　◆　　◆

The next day is the maharajah of Ajeebgarh's birthday, which is celebrated as a state holiday, with a flag raising on the parade ground, a twelve-gun salute and speeches by government officials and other dignitaries. Sikander's father wears his dress uniform with a freshly starched turban. All of the schools and shops are closed. As part of the ceremonies, a new four-anna postage stamp is released, with a portrait of Maharajah Lajawab Singh II. Remembering what his father had told him, Sikander wonders how something as insignificant as a four-anna stamp could lead to war with the British.

After watching the bands and soldiers marching in formation, Sikander meets his friend Lawrence on the steps leading down to the Magor River. The two of them often go fishing in the slow green waters, but today Lawrence has come armed with a new catapult. He is taking target practice at things that go floating past on the sluggish current—a stick that looks like a snake, a turtle that disappears as soon as he shoots in its direction, a wicker basket bobbing on the current. Occasionally there are crocodiles in the water and river dolphins, as well as a fish called a goonch, which is also known as a freshwater shark. When Sikander arrives, Lawrence shows him the slingshot.

"I made it myself," he says.

Sikander admires the catapult with the smooth polished Y of wood. He pulls the rubber thongs and snaps it once.

"I've got something to show you too," he says, reaching into the cloth bag slung over his shoulder.

Lawrence shrugs when he takes the bottle from Sikander, unimpressed. "So? It's an empty gripe-water bottle . . . So what?"

"I found it floating near the railway bridge," says Sikander, taking the scroll of paper from his pocket. "This was in it."

After he reads the message, Lawrence begins to laugh. "It can't be true. Somebody's pulling your leg."

"How do you know?" says Sikander.

"If you found it in this river, then it must have floated downstream. It couldn't come from the sea," says Lawrence, picking up a stone and firing his catapult again. "As far as I know there aren't any desert islands upriver from here."

"Look on the other side. It's some kind of notice, but the dates are in the future, a hundred years from now."

Lawrence studies it carefully, then shakes his head.

"I've read *Great Expectations*," he says, "but this doesn't make any sense . . ."

Sikander takes the bottle back and holds it up to the sunlight. The brilliant blue color of the glass seems magical. Though he has no explanation for the message, the bottle emits a mysterious aura that makes him want to believe in the message he has found.

"I've already written a reply and put it in the bottle. Let's see what happens if I throw it back in the river," Sikander suggests. "Eventually, it should float out to sea."

Lawrence gives another skeptical laugh.

"Go ahead," he says, "but you're wasting your time. It will probably take a hundred years to get a reply, and who knows if the bottle will ever reach this person Gil. Even if he is a castaway, you're not going be able to help him."

"But I can't just ignore it," says Sikander with a shrug. "And there's no harm in writing back, is there?"

The letter he has composed is in English, just as Ghulam Rusool, the calligrapher, taught him:

Sikander Khan
Masala Bazaar
Ajeebgarh—India

5 Nov. 1896

Dear Gil Mendelson—Finch,

If you are actually stranded on a desert island, send us some proof and I will try to *help you. Please also explain the dates on the paper you sent. How can it be 2007?*

I am, sincerely yours,
Sikander

Making sure the cork is tightly in place, Sikander hurls the bottle out into the river. With a splash, it goes under briefly, then bobs to the surface. Lawrence immediately picks up a stone and takes aim with his catapult.

"Hey, don't do that!" Sikander blurts out, shoving his friend's shoulder so the stone misses its target. Before Lawrence can respond, the strangest thing happens. The bottle is surrounded by a dazzling purple halo, like a peacock's feather of light. The intensity increases for several seconds before it disappears completely, as if swallowed by an invisible crocodile.

"What was that!?" says Lawrence, staring at Sikander in alarm.

"I don't know, but it wasn't just gripe water," says Sikander, his eyes scanning the muddy current as it flows downstream.

9

An Edict in the Basement

With one hand, Gil pressed a blank sheet of paper against the wall. In his other hand, he clutched a piece of charcoal. His grandfather held the opposite corner of the paper and shone a flashlight. It was dark and damp inside the cellar, more like a cave or dungeon than the basement of a house. Sections of the floor were dirt. At other places slate flagstones had been arranged in a loose pattern. The only light from outside filtered through two narrow windows at ground level that were coated with grime and cobwebs. The basement smelled of wet earth and mold.

Prescott had insisted that Gil see the basement of the Yankee Mahal, to prove that the stones out of which it was built had come from India. Following his grandfather down a narrow staircase, Gil edged past a stack of wooden crates and boxes, as well as a wine rack full of empty bottles. In one corner stood an oil furnace and boiler. Whenever the furnace ignited, there was a roaring noise and the pipes hissed.

Against one wall lay an old bicycle covered in dust, with flat tires and a wicker basket on the front.

"You're welcome to use this if you'd like," Prescott had said, brushing off the seat. "It's a perfectly good bike. I used it for thirty years until my knees gave out."

Along the ceiling were all kinds of pipes and electric cables. Cans of paint and brushes as well as an antique barbecue cluttered up one corner of the cellar. Prescott had cleared away a couple of broken chairs, then run his hand over the rough foundation of the Yankee Mahal.

"All of these were ballast stones from Ezekiel's ships," he said.

Gil could barely see the walls, except where the flashlight caught the rough edges. Some rocks were smooth and others looked as if they had been chipped and chiseled into shape.

"Here you go," said Prescott, his fingers finding something on the surface of the basement wall. They had positioned the sheet of paper over the stone, which was about a foot square.

"What do I do?" Gil asked.

"Just rub the charcoal over the paper, as if you were coloring it in . . . evenly, but not too hard," Prescott said.

As Gil began to darken the surface of the paper with charcoal, there wasn't much to see at first, except for the uneven texture of the rock. Then suddenly he noticed a few characters emerge, contrasting shapes and lines beneath the sooty layer of charcoal. As he filled the rest of the paper in, he could see three lines of writing in a language he didn't recognize. Each of the lines was broken off, where the stone ended, a cryptic fragment chiseled into the rock.

"What is it?" he asked his grandfather.

"An imperial edict written more than two thousand years ago," said Prescott.

"Can you read it?" Gil asked, removing the paper from the wall and holding it under the flashlight beam.

His grandfather shook his head. "No, it's in an ancient Indian language that isn't used anymore. I've had a couple of scholars look at it. They think it must be part of a proclamation written by the Indian emperor Ashoka, around 250 BC. These edicts were erected at the boundaries of his empire."

"That's so cool. How did it get here?"

"This must have been part of a larger rock on which the edict was carved. It probably came from the eastern coast of India. Somebody broke it into pieces, or maybe it just eroded. By coincidence, the stone fragments were used as ballast in Ezekiel's ships a hundred and fifty years ago."

Gil stared in amazement at the crooked letters on the

paper. It was like seeing the ghost of a dead language that he had rubbed off the stone.

"It's a message of peace and nonviolence," Prescott went on to explain. "Almost all of Ashoka's edicts forbid the killing of living things. He wrote his edicts after a terrible battle in which thousands of men died at a place called Kalinga. When Ashoka saw the destruction of war, he decided never to shed blood again."

"Are there any more inscriptions?" Gil asked, peering into the shadows of the cellar.

"No," said Prescott. "Not that I can find. It's possible that other fragments are hidden in the rocks, though we'd have to take the whole house apart to find them. But there's one other thing I'll show you."

Picking his way through the stack of paint cans and empty crates, Prescott moved aside a couple of boards piled against the wall. Once again, he helped Gil position another blank sheet of paper over a foundation stone. This one was smoother, with a more polished surface. As Gil began to rub the charcoal, a geometric shape appeared. Instead of words, he saw the design of an eight-pointed star, made of two squares overlapping. At the center of the star was a symbol that looked like a stick figure with horns. When he finished rubbing, Gil pulled the sheet of paper away from the wall and squinted at the stone. Although the pattern on the paper was clear and unmistakable, he could barely make out the chiseled shapes on the dark surface of the rock. Yet, as he traced their outlines with one finger, the emblem was etched in his mind.

"The symbol of Mercury," Prescott explained, "the smallest planet in our solar system. In mythology, Mercury is the mischievous messenger of the night sky and conductor of the dead. The Egyptians called him Hap. The Babylonians called him Nabu. In Hindu mythology, he's known as Budha or Naradha. For the Greeks he was Hermes, who carried a winged staff entwined with two serpents. That symbol was adapted by the Romans, who called him Mercury."

"Why's it carved on this stone?" Gil asked.

Prescott shook his head. "I wish I knew the answer to that," he said. "It doesn't seem to have any connection to the edict, and none of the scholars I've consulted can explain why it's here, except that Roman traders came to India in the first century BC. One of them may have carved it on this stone."

10
Bad Luck

Today had been the worst day of Nargis's life. When she got up in the morning she couldn't find the clothes she wanted to wear. After she finally decided on a sweatshirt and jeans, she spilled orange juice on herself during breakfast and had to change again. Then her bicycle had a flat tire, so she had to walk to school and got there late. Her homeroom teacher scolded her for coming in after the bell. During her second period social studies class, Nargis flunked a pop quiz. Later, she went to get a drink and the water fountain sprayed all over her. And in PE, she got hit in the face playing dodgeball and her nose began to bleed. When she went to the infirmary, the nurse wasn't there and she waited in the hall with blood dripping all over her clothes. But the final straw was at lunch, when the only vegetarian food in the cafeteria was tofu burgers and green Jell-O, which Nargis hated. Right after she got her food, somebody tripped her in the line. She dropped her tray on the floor and everyone laughed at her. About that time, Nargis remembered the chain letter and wondered if this was happening to her because of the curse.

When school was finally over, Nargis walked over to Gil's house. She hadn't been able to talk to anyone about the skeletal hand, and it was still bothering her. Her friends at school would never have believed her, and she knew it was better to keep it to herself. When Nargis arrived at the Yankee Mahal, Gil was only too glad to go for a walk. He'd been stuck indoors all day. After showing him the edict in the cellar, his grandfather had given him an old history book to read. ("To further your education," Prescott had said.) It was so boring, Gil kept falling asleep.

He and Nargis took Kipling with them to the park, though this time the dog stayed on the leash.

"I wonder if we should go back to the town dump and have another look," said Nargis. "Maybe the hand is back in the mailbox."

"Probably not," said Gil.

"You definitely saw it, didn't you?" said Nargis, trying to reassure herself.

"Of course," said Gil. "We both saw it. And we smelled it too."

They were quiet for a while, walking across the park. Finally Nargis spoke.

"Why aren't you in school?" she asked, once they'd crossed the hill and were heading toward the ice pond.

"I got kicked out," said Gil.

For a few seconds Nargis didn't say anything.

"From where?"

"McCauley Prep," he said. "It's a snotty boarding school in Connecticut. Anyway, I didn't like it there."

"What grade are you in?"

"Seventh."

"So am I," said Nargis.

"My parents want to put me in another prep school, but if I miss too much, I might have to repeat a year," Gil said, kicking a leaf on the grass.

"Why did you get expelled?" Nargis asked.

Gil looked away, toward the flock of geese.

"Plagiarism," he said.

"Really?"

"Yeah, I was supposed to write a poem but I left it until it was too late. The night before it was due, I looked up some random poetry online and copied it. I know I shouldn't have done it—a dumb idea, but that's what happened . . ." Gil shrugged.

"And they threw you out of school for that?" said Nargis. "Wouldn't they have suspended you or given you a warning first?"

"McCauley Prep makes a big deal about academic honesty," said Gil. "At first they were going to have this whole hearing and make me answer questions, but I said, 'Look. I cheated. I admit it. I won't do it again.' I thought maybe if I was honest about what I'd done, they'd give me a break. But the headmaster told me plagiarism is a crime against literature . . . as if it were something like murder. Anyway, it's over and I'm glad to be out of there."

"What was the poem?" Nargis asked.

"It's by Lewis Carroll, from *Through the Looking-Glass.* I guess I should have known my teacher might recognize it:

> '"*In winter, when the fields are white,*
> *I sing this song for your delight—*
>
> "*In spring when woods are getting green,*
> *I'll try and tell you what I mean—*
>
> "*In summer, when the days are long,*
> *Perhaps you'll understand this song:*
>
> "*In autumn, when the leaves are brown,*
> *Take pen and ink, and write it down.*"'

"You memorized it?" said Nargis.

"There's no way I'll ever forget it now," said Gil. "Those lines are stuck in my head."

By this time, they had reached the ice pond. While Kipling sniffed at the goose dung by the shore, they could see trout feeding on the surface. The water was dimpled at places, almost as if it were starting to rain.

"So, where are you from?" said Gil, trying to change the subject.

"Here," said Nargis. "Carville."

"No, I mean, originally?"

"I was born in America, but my parents came from India."

"That's cool."

"I guess," said Nargis. "Sometimes people just can't figure it out. One of my teachers thought I was adopted. Others talk to me as if I don't speak English. And of course, nobody can pronounce my name."

"Naar-giss," said Gil.

"That's pretty close."

"What does it mean?" he asked.

She made a face. "It means 'narcissus.' But my parents chose it because it's the name of a famous Indian movie star."

"There's nothing wrong with Nargis," said Gil.

"I don't like it. Parents always choose the stupidest names. It isn't fair."

"Well, maybe you could shorten it, like me."

"What's your full name?" she said.

Gil picked up a stone and skipped it across the surface of the pond, scaring the geese.

"Forget it," he said.

"Come on!"

"Okay, but this is embarrassing," he said. "You see, my mother spent a year abroad in France when she was in college, so she thinks she's très European. She named me Gilbert—pronounced 'Jill-bear.' I changed it before I got to kindergarten, but sometimes she still tries to call me that."

"Jill-bear," said Nargis, laughing.

"You see, I shouldn't have told you," said Gil.

"Don't worry, I promise I won't call you that again," she said, trying to keep a straight face.

Suddenly, without any warning, Kipling began to bark and started straining at the leash, his hackles raised. Gil almost fell over before he steadied himself and pulled Kip back. The flock of geese took to the air in alarm, their wings beating together like muffled applause.

"What is it?" said Gil, holding Kip's leash with both hands as the dog kept barking.

"Look over there," said Nargis, pointing toward a line of leafless trees. "Somebody walking . . ."

Gil peered across the park, but all he could see was a shadowy figure disappearing into the gray blur of tree trunks and bare branches.

"Who was it?" he asked.

Nargis shook her head. "It looked like a postman," she said, "carrying a bag. But why would he be here?"

11
Trout Fishing

A rough dirt path zigzags up the ridge through an undulating maze of neatly trimmed tea bushes. Sikander and Lawrence pass groups of pickers with bamboo baskets strapped to their backs. The two boys carry their fishing rods, and Lawrence has a satchel slung over one shoulder. It is warm, even at eight in the morning. A few tall trees, most of their branches trimmed, grow amidst the garden but offer little shade. Half a mile on ahead, they can see where the jungle begins, a dense, wild wall of foliage that rises up steeply to the crest of the ridge.

"I bet I can get to the forest before you!" says Lawrence, starting to run.

"Hey!" Sikander shouts after him. "You're cheating. You got a head start!" He chases after Lawrence. Even though his friend has a ten-yard lead, Sikander begins to catch up. Racing along the path, they come to a series of switchbacks that zigzag up to the boundary of the tea estate. Instead of following the trail, Sikander scrambles straight up the hill. He nearly drops his fishing rod but gets ahead of Lawrence and reaches the trees first.

"Now look who's cheating," Lawrence yells. Both of them are laughing and gasping for breath.

Sikander sits down on a tree root as Lawrence takes out his canteen. He has a drink of water, then passes it to his friend. Looking down across the expanse of tea gardens, he can just make out the red tin roof of his home, a bungalow built on a spur of the ridge overlooking the Magor River. Beyond this lie the white domes of the maharajah's palace and the rooftops of Ajeebgarh. Much farther off, in the distance, they can see the British encampment, line upon line of tents and columns of smoke.

"Do you think there's going to be a war?" Sikander asks in a serious voice.

"My father says there might be," Lawrence answers, "unless the maharajah agrees to the British demands."

"What do they want him to do?" Sikander takes another sip of water.

"He's supposed to remove his picture from the postage stamps," said Lawrence. "You can only have pictures of Queen Victoria, the Empress of India. But my father says that's just an excuse. They're actually worried about the Russians. Supposedly they're trying to negotiate for all the tea from Ajeebgarh to go to Moscow."

"It looks as if there's enough tea for everyone," Sikander says, scanning the gardens below. Putting the canteen back in his satchel, Lawrence gets to his feet and continues up the ridge. Now that the path winds its way through the shadows of the trees, it is cooler. There are birdcalls overhead, the noisy cackle of hornbills and the persistent, maddening cry of a brain fever bird.

Half an hour later, Sikander and Lawrence cross a saddle of the ridge, from where they can see a tiny lake called Ambital, cupped in a hollow of the ridge. It's shaped like a paisley design, rounded at one end and tapering to a curlicue where a mountain stream flows out of a ravine.

Sikander pauses to see if any trout are feeding. Lawrence points to a couple of dimples on the surface of the water, but mostly it is still, a watery mirror reflecting the surrounding trees and ridges. As the boys make their way to the water's edge, they come upon a rectangular slab of marble, a tombstone covered with lichens and moss. Lawrence kneels down and runs his fingers over the carved letters.

Sacred

to the memory of

EZEKIEL FINCH

March 12, 1802—August 18, 1879

Come live with mee, and bee my love,
And wee will some new pleasures prove
Of golden sands and christall brookes,
With silken lines, and silver hookes.

John Donne

Grass and ground orchids frame the lonely tombstone. Sikander picks up his fishing rod and checks the knot that holds the hook. Lawrence chooses a brass flyspoon from his tackle box and ties it on. He knows there are trout in the lake, but the last two times they have come here, the boys have gone home empty-handed. His father has suggested he try some other kind of bait—crickets or worms—but Lawrence is sure that sooner or later the gleaming brass spoon and red feather will attract a trout. Stepping up to the water's edge, he casts into the center of the pond. Meanwhile, Sikander has brought a ball of dough that he squeezes in his palm. He then breaks off a pinch to put on the hook. Moving up the bank a ways, Sikander tosses the baited hook into the clear water and sits down to wait.

Three hours later Sikander has caught four trout and Lawrence has two. Around noon the boys set off down the hill, carrying their fish. Neither of them has had breakfast, and both are starving. Lawrence's face is badly sunburned, almost as bright red as his curly hair.

"My father told me these fish came all the way from America," he says.

"How?" Sikander asks in disbelief. "Did they swim here?"

"No. Ezekiel Finch, the man whose gravestone we saw by the lake, brought the trout eggs with him by ship. He built a fish hatchery here at Ambital forty years ago and stocked the lake."

Sikander is about to reply, but all at once, three men step out of the trees and block the path. Two are carrying guns and the third has a sword. All of them are Europeans. The clothes they wear are soldiers' uniforms—red coats with rickrack and bandoliers. But these are filthy and torn.

"'Ello!" says the tallest of the three, in a menacing voice. He is unshaven, with bloodshot eyes. "What have we 'ere?"

Lawrence and Sikander stop in their tracks.

"They've caught some trout!" says the second man, who is short and squat, with one black eye and a broken tooth. He holds his sword in one hand.

"Who are you?" says Lawrence, trying to sound brave but with a quaver in his voice.

"We're soldiers, laddie. Can't y' see?" says the third man with a wicked laugh. "Three British Tommies are we. Tommy-one. Tommy-two. And Tommy-three. From the Duke of Dumbarton's own Third Foot. And we're hungry too."

Sikander can tell these aren't ordinary soldiers. They look more like criminals. Tommy-one points the barrel of his musket at Sikander.

"We'll take those fish, if y' please," he demands, his voice a snarl.

"You can't have them," says Lawrence. "They're ours!"

The three Tommies look at one another seriously for a moment, then break into loud guffaws.

"And who's going to stop us, laddie?"

"My father," says Lawrence, turning even redder than he was before. "Mr. Roderick Sleeman. He owns the tea estate, just down the path from here. He'll call the police."

"Will 'e, now?" says Tommy-one.

"How interesting," says Tommy-two.

"Blimey!" says Tommy-three. "I'd love a cuppa tea. Is 'e rich, your father?"

Sikander is about to stop Lawrence from answering, but his friend blurts out, "Yes, of course he is. He's a lot richer than you."

"Then maybe we'll take more than just the trout . . . ," says Tommy-one, an evil glint in his eye.

Before Lawrence can move, Tommy-two steps forward and grabs him with one hand, holding the sword to his neck.

"What do we do with the other one?" says Tommy-three.

"Shoot 'im."

"Naw. A waste of powder."

Tommy-three snatches the fish.

"Let my friend go!" Sikander shouts.

"Oy! Blister my kidneys! He speaks the Queen's Inglish," says Tommy-two.

"I suppose your father isn't rich as well, is 'e?"

Sikander glares at him, but Tommy-three presses the blade of his sword against Lawrence's throat.

"Not by the look of 'im," says Tommy-one. "Get lost. Go on, before I blow yer brains out."

Sikander doesn't want to abandon his friend, but maybe if he runs for help, he might be able to save Lawrence from these men. Before Sikander has any more time to think, Tommy-one puts the barrel of his musket to his chest.

"Go tell your friend's rich father that we want a thousand

rupees ransom. Tell 'im we'll be in touch," says Tommy-one. "We'll be sending a letter to Mr. Roderick Sleeman, Esquire."

Dropping his fishing tackle, Sikander races down the hill, through the forest and out into the tea estate. Running as fast as he can, he reaches the planter's bungalow, where he gasps out the news that Lawrence has been kidnapped.

12
Rattle Beach

With all of the excitement of the skeletal hand, Gil had forgotten completely about the bottle he had thrown back into the sea. But now, as he tried to puzzle through everything that was taking place, he suddenly remembered the bright blue color of the glass, as if it had drifted into his memory again. After Nargis had gone home, Gil slipped out the kitchen door again and headed down the trail to Rattle Beach. By now the bottle was probably lying at the bottom of the Atlantic, or maybe it had washed on down the coast, but Gil felt an irresistible urge to find out if it was still there.

Sure enough, as soon as he scrambled down the rocks onto the shingle beach, he saw the blue shape bobbing in the water, ten feet from shore. The tide was in and the waves kept splashing up onto the rocks. Gil didn't want to get wet, but he had no choice. He took off his shoes and socks, then rolled his jeans up to his knees.

When he stepped into the water, it felt as if his toes and ankles had been grabbed by claws of ice. The blue bottle rocking on the waves beckoned to him. Shivering with cold, he waded out into the surf, no longer caring if his jeans got wet. An incoming wave almost knocked him off his feet, which were completely numb by now. At the last minute he reached out and caught the bottle by its neck. Floundering back to shore, Gil rubbed his legs and feet until the circulation began to return, then put on his socks and shoes, even though he was soaking wet. He could see a message in the bottle and wanted to open it right there, but forced himself to wait until he got home to the Yankee Mahal.

Prescott was in the kitchen, opening a can of chicken stew for dinner.

"Where did you disappear to?" he asked as Gil came in.

"Nowhere. I just went down to the beach."

Seeing how his jeans were wet, Prescott raised a questioning eyebrow but didn't say any more as Gil headed upstairs. Once he was safely in his room, he uncorked the bottle and shook the message out onto the bed. He could see it wasn't the same scrap of paper he had sent but a reply in a careful, deliberate hand from someone he'd never heard of before: Sikander Khan. Ajeebgarh. 5 November 1896. Yesterday. But 112 years ago!

Just then, he heard a knock at the door. Though Gil was able to hide the message in his pocket, the blue bottle stood on his bedside table when Prescott came in.

"Are you all right?" his grandfather asked.

"I'm fine," Gil said.

"How'd you get wet?"

Gil looked around and saw the bottle. He shrugged, deciding there wasn't any harm in telling half the truth.

"I found this down on Rattle Beach. It's pretty cool."

When he handed the bottle to his grandfather, Prescott held it up, admiring the color, then turned it toward the light, so he could read the molded lettering.

"A. K. Jaddoowalla's Finest Indian Gripe Water."

"What does that mean?" asked Gil.

"It's a mild kind of medicine that's given to young children who suffer from colic," said Prescott. "I remember we used to give it to your mother when she was a baby."

"Colic?" Gil asked.

"Stomach cramps. Nothing serious, but your mother would howl and cry a lot. Gripe water is made with anise, and it used to calm your mother down right away."

"I guess I just like the color of the bottle," said Gil. "It kind of has a glow about it."

Gil nearly told his grandfather about the message he'd sent and the answer he'd got, but he decided to wait until he had more proof of what was going on.

Later that night, after dinner, he wrote a reply:

Gil Mendelson-Finch
The Yankee Mahal
Carville, MA 02453

Hi Sikander,

Writing a letter to somebody living over a
hundred years ago seems kind of weird, but

a lot of strange things have been happening to me. I don't know what to believe anymore.

The truth is, I'm not really stranded on a desert island. (Sorry about that.) I'm living with my grandfather in a house that was built by somebody named Ezekiel Finch, who traveled to India in 1840. He was an ancestor of mine. I'm not sure what else to tell you about myself, except that I've been thrown out of school and I just met a girl named Nargis whose family comes from India, originally.

You asked me for some kind of proof. I'm sending you a newspaper clipping from the CARVILLE GAZETTE with today's date on it. Maybe you could send me something like that, just so we're sure that all of this is really happening.

Okay. Take it easy,
Gil

13

The Postmaster's Tale

When Prescott suggested they go to the post office the next day, Gil tried to think up some excuse, but he didn't have anything better to do. As far as he was concerned, a post office had to be the most boring place in the world. By that time, he'd already taken Kip for a walk to Rattle Beach, where he'd thrown the gripe-water bottle back into the sea. Rather than hang around at home, Gil decided to keep his grandfather company and go along for the ride. The post office in Carville was on Wordsworth Street, near the town green. It was a redbrick building with white trim and a flagpole in front.

"I always enjoy a trip to the post office," said Prescott, as if he'd read his grandson's mind. "People complain about the time it takes to mail a letter, but I don't mind standing in line, even during the Christmas rush, or waiting for someone to fill out a form."

"Why don't you use e-mail?" said Gil.

"Too fast for me," said Prescott. "I like to savor the time

between posting a letter and getting a reply. There's also something about words on paper that's much more satisfying than a phone call or messages on a computer screen. I like the feeling of opening an envelope and not knowing exactly what's written inside."

Gil raised a skeptical eyebrow, but left it at that. When they entered the main door, Prescott pointed out a photograph of the old post office, which had burned down in 1951. The new building had been constructed on the same site, though it faced in a different direction. Along one wall were lines of postboxes. Opposite this were the counters and vending machine for stamps, as well as racks of envelopes and forms. The postmaster's office was at the back, near the delivery and sorting rooms.

"I come here at least three times a week," said Prescott. He was carrying a couple of letters and bills to mail. Instead of buying postage from the vending machine, he went to the counter and started talking with one of the clerks. Gil wandered over to the bulletin board, which had a display of new stamps with pictures of movie stars he didn't recognize, the American flag and cartoon characters. He wished he'd stayed at home.

After mailing his letters, Gil's grandfather gestured for him to follow him into the postmaster's office, where a heavyset man with gold-rimmed glasses was sitting behind a desk piled with papers.

"Good morning, Fred," said Prescott. "I wanted to introduce my grandson. Gil, this is Mr. Dougherty."

The postmaster reached across the desk and shook hands.

"Have a seat," he said. "Cup of coffee?"

"No thanks," said Prescott. "I just dropped in to ask you a question. You've heard the story of the unknown postman, haven't you?"

Fred seemed startled, then nodded. "Sure."

"How much truth is there in the tale?"

"Truth?" said Fred with a laugh. "In a ghost story? Are you kidding? It's nonsense! Don't tell me you're starting to believe in ghosts, Prescott."

Gil suddenly got interested, leaning forward in his chair and listening carefully.

"No, of course not, but I've been thinking of writing a poem about the unknown postman," said Prescott. "Firemen and soldiers get all the glory, but letter carriers are unsung heroes. They deserve to be memorialized too."

"That's true," Fred agreed.

"So, I wanted some details," Prescott said, looking sidelong at his grandson. "Even if it's a folktale, the story of the unknown postman must have some basis in fact."

Fred took off his glasses and rubbed his eyes, then turned to Gil. "Do you believe in ghosts?"

Gil shook his head. "I don't think so."

"Neither do I, but a lot of people seem to accept the supernatural . . ." Fred had a slow way of talking that made Gil squirm with impatience. "They say the unknown postman walks around Carville, carrying dead letters. You know, the kind that can't be

67

delivered. Either the numbers and street names don't match or there's no return address. It could be someone's moved without leaving forwarding instructions . . ."

When he paused, Gil was about to mention the strange figure he and Nargis had seen two days ago, but he decided not to interrupt the postmaster's story.

Prescott prompted Fred. "Go on. Who was he?"

"He doesn't have a name," the postmaster continued. "Some say he walked a rural delivery route between the farms that lay on the outskirts of Hornswoggle Bay. But we don't have any records and I wasn't here back then . . ." When he paused, it seemed as if he'd forgotten what he was talking about, twirling a pencil between his fingers.

"Do you know how he died?" Gil asked.

"Not for sure. There's so much rumor mixed with facts," said Fred, now playing with the paper clips on his desk. "It's just a tall tale—make-believe—part of the postal lore of these parts."

"We'd like to hear it anyway," Prescott said.

"Well . . ." Fred took a deep breath. "Supposedly, he was killed when the old post office burned down in 1951. He got burned up with all of the letters. Went up in smoke, along with all of the Christmas cards and other mail. The fire happened on December twentieth. Everything was destroyed, right down to the foundations. Not a trace of the postman either, though people said they saw him inside, flailing his arms and trying to put out the flames. Even the firemen claimed he died in the blaze, though they couldn't find any of his remains when they sifted through the ashes.

"There were all sorts of rumors about letters that got lost—checks for thousands of dollars burned up in the fire, Christmas packages with expensive gifts. A lot of false insurance claims were filed. Someone demanded compensation for a diamond ring they'd sent in the mail, but there wasn't any sign of it, or any receipt. Again, I wasn't around to witness any of this; it's all hearsay. All of the records and files got destroyed as well, so there's no way to prove who the postman was. Some people believe he set the fire himself because he was upset with the postmaster. They say he pretended to fight the fire, then ran away. Others claimed he died trying to save the mail. Whether he's the villain or the hero of this story, it's hard to say."

"But somebody must have known who he was," Gil said, putting his elbows on the postmaster's desk.

Fred shook his head. "From what I've heard, he had no family or friends. Over the years, people have suggested we put up a plaque for him, you know, like the unknown soldier."

"You've never seen him?" Prescott asked.

"No, of course not!" Fred shuffled some of the papers on his desk. "I told you, I don't believe in ghosts. But four days after the fire in 1951, it snowed. A white Christmas. The burned-down remains of the post office were covered in white, like a shroud. People said the next morning, all along the mail route the unknown postman used to walk, there were sooty footprints, the shape of a man's shoe in the snow, outlined with a dusting of ash. That's how the story started. Some people still believe he walks his route, trying to deliver the letters and cards destroyed in the fire. Some say they've seen him passing through the older neighborhoods of Carville at dusk. And whenever we have a white Christmas, there are reports of ashy footprints in the snow."

14

Par Avian

THE AJEEBGARH TIMES

TEA PLANTER'S SON KIDNAPPED
By Our Crime Correspondent

AJEEBGARH, 8/11/1896. A brazen kidnapping occurred yesterday, when Lawrence Sleeman, the son of Mr. Roderick Sleeman, was taken captive along the footpath that runs from Upper Finch tea estate to Ambital. Reports indicate that the kidnappers are army deserters from the British military encampment on the borders of Ajeebgarh.

Mr. Sleeman and the police have appealed to the public for any information leading to the recovery of his son. No ransom note has been received from the kidnappers and their whereabouts are unknown. A reward of rupees 1,000 has been offered by

H. H. Maharajah Lajawab Singh II for any clues leading to the arrest of these criminals.

Sikander tears the front-page article out of the newspaper and puts it inside the blue bottle, along with a note to Gil telling him about the kidnapping.

After throwing it in the river, he returns home to find a police inspector, from the Royal Constabulary of Ajeebgarh, waiting to question him. This is the third time he's been interrogated. The inspector is suspicious at first, assuming that Sikander may have been associated with the kidnappers. But when he hears a description of the three men who took Lawrence hostage, the policeman nods and strokes his whiskers with a grave look on his face.

"They called themselves the three Tommies," says Sikander, "and they talk as if they have toffees stuck in their teeth."

"Aaah," says the police inspector. "Deserters from the army. The Duke of Dumbarton's own Third Foot. Wanted men. Ruthless brigands who were facing a court-martial."

"They said they would be writing a ransom note to Mr. Sleeman," Sikander continues.

The policeman raises his bushy eyebrows. "We'll send out a search party to look for them, but who knows where they've gone. They didn't give any indication, did they?"

Sikander shakes his head helplessly.

"You will find Lawrence, won't you, sir?" he asks, trying to hold back his tears. "They're not going to hurt him, are they?"

"We hope not," says the policeman. "But these are desperate men. They've killed before. They'll kill again."

Over the next week, Sikander goes to the police station every day and asks about Lawrence, but there is no news. Search parties have scoured the hills above Ajeebgarh, but all they find are the ashes of a campfire and the bones of six trout. No other sign of the army deserters or their hostage can be found.

Though he collects lampblack each morning, and mixes ink after school, Sikander cannot forget the loss of his friend. He feels guilty for having abandoned Lawrence, even if the Tommies gave him no choice. Sometimes he becomes so upset his tears fall into the ink and dilute the mixture. The letter writer grumbles at him.

"Not the right shade of black," he says. "What's wrong? Have you forgotten everything I taught you?"

Sikander snuffles into his sleeve and adds more soot and resin until the ink is the correct color and consistency—as dark as his mood.

An old woman has come to dictate a letter to her son. Her message is full of family gossip and rambles on for several pages. Sikander feels frustrated listening to the woman, thinking there are so many more important things that could be written. When it's finished, the letter is folded into an envelope and sealed. Sikander is told to carry it to the post office and make sure it is mailed to Calcutta. This time, he doesn't leap to his feet but walks slowly, dejectedly through the crowded lane, head held low.

"What's wrong with you?" asks the postal clerk when Sikander hands him the letter. "Such a long face!"

"My friend has been kidnapped," he explains. "I'm afraid he'll be killed."

From his stool behind the counter, the clerk peers down at Sikander sympathetically before he weighs the letter.

"There haven't been any letters for Mr. Sleeman at the tea estate, have there?" Sikander asks. "We're waiting for a ransom note."

The clerk shakes his head, then checks the envelope. "First class to Calcutta . . . Three ounces . . . Two annas."

Sikander hands over the coins and listens to the thump, thump as the clerk cancels the stamp. It sounds like a judge's hammer, punctuating a fatal verdict.

When Sikander returns to the letter writer's shop, he finds that Ghulam Rusool has gone out for his afternoon walk. Picking up the pen and choosing a blank sheet of paper, Sikander dips the nib in a bottle of ink. Maybe if he writes to Lawrence, something might happen, though he knows there is no address to which his message can be sent.

Dear Lawrence,

Don't be afraid. The police are searching for you. I'm sure they will rescue you very soon. Please don't think I was a coward to run away. I didn't want to leave you but I had no choice. Now I wish I'd stayed with you or let them kidnap me instead. We're waiting for the ransom note but nothing has reached your father yet. I'm sure he'll pay the money as soon as he can and make the Tommies set you free.

I am your friend,
Sikander

As soon as he finishes writing the note, Sikander has an idea. He hurries home and climbs to the roof of his house. Taking one of the pigeons from the coop, he rolls the note around its leg and ties it with a piece of string. Then he tosses the bird into the air and watches it fly away, high into the air, circling once, then disappearing into the clouds.

15

Lenore

There were a lot of things Gil didn't know about his grandfather, until he moved into the Yankee Mahal. One of them was that Prescott had a girlfriend. Her name was Lenore Sullivan and she lived in Houghton-on-Waspanoag, just across the bay from Carville. It was a much more exclusive town, with a yacht club and palatial homes. Lenore's house was smaller than most, set off by itself on a spit of land near the mouth of the Waspanoag River. There was a broad beach in front with clam flats at low tide and sand dunes fringed with poverty grass.

The day after Gil and Nargis discovered the skeletal hand, Lenore invited Prescott and his grandson over to dinner. Gil felt self-conscious meeting her at first, but his grandfather reassured him.

"Don't worry," he said. "Lenore is one of the most easygoing people you'll ever meet. She has to be if she's put up with me for fifteen years. Of course, she's also borderline cuckoo."

"What do you mean?" Gil asked as they drove along the coastal road.

"You'll see," said Prescott.

When they crossed a stone bridge over the Waspanoag River and arrived at the gate to Lenore's house, there was a sign posted out front with purple and green lettering.

PSYCHIC YOGA
THERAPEUTIC MASSAGE
FORTUNE-TELLING
WANT TO KNOW YOUR FUTURE
OR YOUR PAST?
JUST ASK LENORE!

Gil and his grandfather exchanged a glance as they drove up to the house, in front of which stood an old station wagon covered in more rust than paint. Gil didn't know what to expect, but as soon as he met Lenore, he liked her. She was only a couple of years younger than Prescott, and her white hair was cut shorter than Gil's. Her glasses seemed to always be slipping down her nose, and she had a natural smile, with lots of tanned wrinkles on her face. Lenore led them through the house to a glassed-in porch facing the ocean. From here they had a view of the beach and could see the Carville lighthouse in the distance.

"I know your grandfather is going to have iced tea, but I'm sure you'd like something else to drink," she said.

Gil shrugged politely.

"Root beer or ginger ale?"

"Ginger ale, please," said Gil.

Lenore smiled again. "I've got a grandson named Martin who lives in New Mexico. He's about your age. Every time I see him, he's grown another inch."

As they sat down, Gil caught sight of a huge Persian cat stepping through the door that opened onto the porch. The furry animal looked like an angora sweater come to life. Lenore snapped her fingers.

"His name is Xerxes," she said as the cat sauntered over to where they sat, tail raised like an ostrich plume. "He's the main reason your grandfather and I can't live together."

Gil looked across at Prescott, who frowned.

"He's got a dog. I've got a cat," Lenore continued. "We tried to introduce them once. Nearly killed each other!"

"Cats and postmen," said Prescott. "The two things Kip can't stand."

Lenore stroked Xerxes' head as he nuzzled her leg.

"Do you have a girlfriend, Gil?" she asked.

The question took him by surprise, and he swallowed his ginger ale quickly before it came out his nose. Then he shook his head.

"Too bad," said Lenore. "We'll have to find someone for you."

"Now, don't get started," Prescott warned. "Leave the poor guy alone. He's got a friend named Nargis."

"Nargis?" said Lenore.

"She's not my girlfriend," said Gil, trying to stop blushing.

Xerxes ambled across and let him scratch behind one ear. The cat's fur felt like brushed silk.

A short while later, just as the sun was setting over the bay, Lenore served dinner—baked cod with green beans, scalloped potatoes and sweet corn. For dessert they had apple pie and ice cream.

"I hope the food's all right," said Lenore. "I don't know what your grandfather has been feeding you."

"It tastes great," said Gil. Then after chewing a bite he asked, "Can you really tell a person's future?"

Lenore laughed. "Of course I can."

"Or so she says . . . ," Prescott added with a wink.

"Your grandfather is the biggest skeptic in the world," said Lenore. "He doesn't believe in anything that lies beyond the end of his nose. I've tried to read his fortune several times, but he refuses. Maybe he's just scared to find out the truth."

"Or maybe I'm just sensible," said Prescott, leaning back in his chair.

"How can you tell someone's fortune?" Gil asked, feeling curious and cautious at the same time.

"Mostly, I look at the lines on the palm of a person's hand, or I read the tea leaves in their cup," said Lenore. "I also interpret horoscopes. My grandmother taught me everything I know. She was a full-blooded Gypsy."

"Maybe you should tell Lenore about the hand," said Prescott, half teasing.

Gil was just getting up to help clear the plates. He could see that Lenore shot his grandfather a glance.

"What sort of hand?" she said.

"Ask Gil," said Prescott. "I didn't see it."

Lenore gave Gil an encouraging look.

"It was a skeleton's hand . . . I guess," he said. "We found it in an old mailbox at the town dump. But when we went back, it was gone."

"Just a hand?" asked Lenore.

"Only the bones," said Gil. "The fingers and thumb. It was cut off at the wrist."

"Did it have a bad smell?" Lenore asked with a serious expression on her face. "Like rotting flowers?"

As soon as she said this, Gil felt as if a bucketful of ice cubes had just been poured down his spine. "How did you guess?"

"It wasn't a guess," she said, pushing her glasses up onto the bridge of her nose. "Despite what your grandfather thinks, I do have a certain clairvoyance for these kinds of things."

"Have you ever seen the hand?" Gil asked.

"No, but I've heard about it . . . ," she said mysteriously. "Come help me clear the table."

Gil followed Lenore into the kitchen. He rinsed the plates as she filled the dishwasher.

"Do you know whose hand it is?" Gil asked. "Was it someone who was murdered?"

Lenore shook her head and smiled.

"Nothing as awful as that. Of course, there are a lot of stories around here about ghosts and spirits, from pirate shipwrecks and that sort of thing. Most of them aren't true." Lenore's voice sounded perfectly normal, as if she were talking about the weather. "But the spinster's hand—that's what it's called—belonged to a woman who died years ago, unmarried . . . alone. A sad sort of story."

"Is the hand dangerous?" said Gil, imagining the bony fingers strangling his throat.

"No, I don't think so," said Lenore with a shrug. "The hand belonged to a woman named Camellia Stubbs. She was in love with your ancestor Ezekiel Finch, who built the Yankee Mahal. Of course, that's not a story your grandfather would have told you, is it? He doesn't believe in these sorts of things. They say the spinster's hand is still searching for her lost lover. Camellia's bony fingers will never rest until she finds Ezekiel's grave, so she can finally clasp his cold, dead hand in hers."

Gil nearly dropped the plate he was rinsing. The thought of two skeletons holding hands creeped him out.

When they returned to the glassed-in porch, Prescott had shifted his chair around to look at the sea. The sky had darkened and the horizon had almost disappeared, but there was one faint speck of light in the sky.

"Look," said Lenore, pointing. "There's Mercury."

Gil could barely see it, a distant glimmer.

"When's your birthday, Gil?" Lenore asked.

"September eighteenth," he answered cautiously.

"So you're a Virgo," Lenore said with a frown, as if she were calculating things in her head. "Your star sign is governed by Mercury, which is in retrograde."

"Don't believe a word she says," Prescott warned him.

"Mercury's just a planet, nothing more. There's no truth in astrology!"

"Come on, don't be so cynical," said Lenore, putting a hand on Prescott's shoulder. "Poets are supposed to be sensitive to the mysteries of the world."

"We also try to tell the truth," Prescott muttered.

"Isn't Mercury the messenger?" Gil asked.

"That's right," said Lenore.

Gil leaned forward. "Like that symbol you showed me, Grandpa. The one that's carved in the basement of the Yankee Mahal . . ."

"Sure," said Prescott. "But that's ancient mythology, stories that someone made up centuries ago to explain the mysteries of nature before scientists discovered the facts about the universe."

"Who knows what's really a fact or not," said Lenore. "Why can't the future be written in the stars?"

"Because it's superstition," said Prescott, waving his hand as if to shoo away a fly.

"What does *retrograde* mean?" asked Gil.

"For the next three weeks, the planet moves backward. If Mercury is in retrograde, it means that things are unsettled and unpredictable," Lenore explained.

"Nonsense," Prescott said. "Mercury isn't moving backward. It's still orbiting around the sun, in the same direction it's gone for millions of years. This business of being retrograde is an optical illusion created by the rotation of the earth. It just looks as if it's going in reverse."

Lenore smiled at him patiently. "Everyone's free to believe what they want," she said, turning to Gil. "How about you? Do you want me to read your palm?"

He hesitated, glancing out the window at the flickering planet. When he nodded, Prescott threw up his hands in dismay.

Pulling her chair forward, Lenore gently took Gil's hand in hers. She turned it toward the light and pressed his fingers together to make the lines and creases stand out more clearly. For several minutes, she studied his palm intently.

"So, what do you see in his future?" Prescott asked with a chuckle.

"We're certainly not going to tell you," said Lenore, "since you're such a cynic."

After a few more seconds, she closed Gil's palm. Then leaning over and cupping one hand around his ear, Lenore whispered what was written on his hand.

16
Dead Letter

Hornswoggle Bay
Sabbath, December 2, 1840

My Dearest Ezekiel,

I do not know where or when this letter will find you. Perhaps in India, if it ever reaches you at all. My only hope is that these pages make their way into your hands and my words can soften your heart. I dare not ask for your forgiveness, or even your understanding. All I can do is try to explain the terrible confusion and loss I have felt since the day you sailed away. From my window, I watched you standing on the deck of the Moorish Queen as the crew cast off. When the clipper's sails filled with the wind, I felt my breath go out of me.

At that moment, I regretted every churlish word I spoke to you these past few weeks.

You must hate me for it, but please know that when I said I could not marry you, because my parents had chosen another man, it was a naïve girl who spoke—an innocent, reckless child, who destroyed the very thing she cherished most. I know it will offer no consolation, nor ease your revulsion for me, but I have broken off my engagement to Edward Muybridge and told my parents that I will never accept any other suitor but you. This I know will be impossible, dear Ezekiel, for I have hurt you deeply and unjustly.

You are the only man I can ever love, but in my foolishness I did not realize it until the moment you set sail for India. My only hope is that someday you will return, so that I can see you riding down the street again. I long for another glimpse of you, as on that first day I saw you arriving at church in your blue serge coat and buckskin boots. How could I have let the disapproval of my family and friends blind me to your love?

Every night I pray that I shall wake up the next morning to see you standing on the foredeck when the clipper returns. But there is no reason I should hope for any such miracle.

When you swore that you would stay away
from Massachusetts for the rest of your life, I
felt as if a door had been shut upon my heart,
a heavy oak door that will outlast us all.

Beloved Ezekiel, I have cut a lock of my
hair and placed it between these pages, so that
you may remember how you twisted it gently
between your fingers that day last spring, when
we rode out to the ice pond near your home. Do
you still recall that morning, or have you cast
all of our precious memories into the sea?

I do not hope for a reply to this letter, even
if it reaches you in that far-off land. But
know that I will love you forever and that no
other man shall ever take this hand of mine
in his.

Farewell, my darling,
Your one true love,
Camellia

More than 150 years after it was written, this letter remains
unopened, these tragic words unread. The handwriting is perfect, each letter clearly formed, but Camellia's plea is never answered because her letter fails to reach its destination. The sheets
of paper that she folded so carefully, and kissed with trembling
lips, remain inside the stiff, unyielding envelope that also contains a curl of her chestnut brown hair, tied with a ribbon cut

from her dress. If only the letter had been delivered to Ezekiel he might have changed his mind, understanding her pain, even as he suffered his own anguish. Reading that she had broken off her engagement, he might have returned to Massachusetts and reclaimed his love.

Instead, the letter is lost. When Camellia hands it to the captain of the *Bride of Capri*, another of Ezekiel's clipper ships, he promises to deliver it to his employer in India. Sadly, the letter disappears during a hurricane off the Cape of Good Hope. Though the captain kept it safely in one of his chests, the violence of the storm overturns his boxes and baggage. The contents spill out onto the floor of the cabin and the letter slides across the polished oak boards that lean and sway with the tumult of the waves. Camellia's letter slips through a gap in the floorboards and drops into a crevice between the ship's hull and the cargo hold, which is filled with blocks of ice covered in sawdust. Though the captain remembers his promise and searches for the letter after the storm, he cannot find it. With every intention of confessing this to Ezekiel, he sails on to Calcutta. A week after reaching port, however, he falls victim to virulent cholera and dies a sudden, delirious death.

These tearful words, which might have reversed the course of love and brought Ezekiel home from India, are entombed within the *Bride of Capri*, which later sinks off Nantucket in 1865.

Yet, the envelope is eventually retrieved—not by scuba divers who search the wreck years later, not by the schools of cod and halibut that feed on scullery scraps from the *Bride of Capri*, nor the lobsters that feast on her crew. Instead, it is recovered by a disembodied cluster of bones that scuttles along the sea floor like a minstrel crab and plucks the letter from the shattered hull. Quick as pincers, the macabre fingers grab Camellia's letter and carry it to shore, where the unknown postman waits. A melancholy figure in his gray blue uniform, he watches with sad eyes as the hand emerges from the receding tide, carrying Camellia's unopened letter.

A fetid whiff of putrid flesh, combined with the scent of lilacs and the briny smell of the sea, accompanies the gruesome hand as it drops the letter in the mailbag. Lifting himself onto weary legs, the aged postman continues on his way. His shoulders slump under the weight he carries, a sack full of dead letters, the heavy burden of messages unread.

17
Texting Through Time

Hi Sikander,

I wish I could do something to help rescue your friend. Maybe, if I climbed inside this bottle, I might be able to travel back in time and help you hunt for Lawrence. But, of course, I can't.

India seems so far away from here. And when I think that you're living a hundred years ago, Ajeebgarh feels even farther away, like another planet in a different galaxy. I keep forgetting that in your time there are so many things that haven't been invented, like television and computers. Of course, living with my grandfather right now, I don't have any of these things myself.

Sometimes I feel as if this bottle is a kind

of instant messenger. Of course, you probably don't know what that is, and I'm not sure if I can explain it. I also can't explain how this bottle works. Do you have any idea why it carries our messages back and forth?

                                    Write again soon.
                                    Gil

Dear Gil,

I got your letter a few minutes ago and am replying immediately. It doesn't seem to take any time at all for this bottle to travel from here to there and back again. I don't know what makes this bottle work, except maybe it's some kind of magic.

    We still don't have any news about Lawrence and I don't want to imagine what has happened to him. His kidnappers are vicious men, and if they don't get a ransom, who knows what they will do. I keep wishing we hadn't gone fishing that day. None of this would have happened. But you can't go back and change things, can you? Of course I know there's nothing you can do to help. By the time you get this letter, a hundred years from now, all of us will probably be dead.

It looks as if there might be a war between Ajeebgarh and the British, who are camped on the outskirts of the city. We can hear them firing their cannons and they are threatening to invade.

You mentioned something called television and computers. I wonder what these things are. Is it like the telegraph, which just came to Ajeebgarh last year?

This time, when I throw the bottle in the river, I'm going to wait and see how long it takes to come back.

Your friend,
Sikander

Hi Sikander,

Your answer arrived right after I wrote to you. Ten minutes ago I tossed this bottle back into the sea. After that I was sitting in the sun, watching a lobsterman checking his traps offshore. Then, just as I was going to head home, the blue bottle popped out of the waves and washed right up to my feet. I guess it must be magic, or some kind of scientific phenomenon that hasn't been discovered yet.

I hope the war doesn't happen. What are you going to do? Why are the British planning to attack Ajeebgarh?

You asked about computers and television. These are machines with screens on which words and pictures travel instantly from one place to another, sort of like this bottle but much more complicated. It's hard to explain because I guess you don't have electricity either.

I have to get home before my grandfather thinks I'm lost, but I'll come here again tomorrow morning to get your reply.

Gil

Dear Gil,

This will have to be a very short note because I must get to work. I'm apprenticed to a calligrapher, who has to write an official proclamation from the maharajah to the

British, asking them to withdraw their troops. If this war happens it will be terrible. It's the stupidest conflict—all because of a postage stamp. The British don't want the maharajah putting his picture on the stamp. They only want the Queen of England, but of course that's just an excuse. I'll write again soon.

Sikander

Hey Sikander,

I hope the British haven't attacked. It does seem pretty dumb to start a war because of a stamp, but I guess a lot of wars have occurred for no reason at all.

Are you working full-time or do you also go to school?

I showed my friend Nargis the last few messages you've sent and she wants to know if your mother cooks bhindi. (I don't know what that is, but she says you'll know.) Nargis wants to write something, so I'll stop . . .

Hi Sikander,

This is Nargis. It's pretty cool that we can write to you like this, but I wish we could help you find your friend. Though my parents come from India, I've been there only once. Just to Delhi where my aunt lives. Maybe next time I go, I'll visit Ajeebgarh. But of course, you won't be there. That seems kind of weird.

Just writing this note, I'm getting creeped out. Hope you're safe, with all of the war and stuff.

Nargis

Dear Gil and Nargis,

Thanks for writing. I was feeling very depressed today because my father, who is one of the maharajah's bodyguards, has been posted to the palace barracks, which means the fighting is going to start soon. We don't know when it will begin, but all of the foreigners who live in Ajeebgarh are leaving, including Lawrence's parents. There doesn't seem to be any chance that he is still alive.

94

Even though I sometimes feel hopeless, your letter cheered me up. Of course I know what bhindi is. My mother cooks it sometimes, though it's not my favorite vegetable. Too slimy. I wish both of you could visit Ajeebgarh—maybe not now, but at some other time (maybe in the future, when all of the fighting is over). Sometimes it's so confusing. For you, all of this is history. You can probably read about it in a book. For me, it's happening right now, today and tomorrow.

Please keep writing. My mother doesn't want me to leave the house, but I sneaked out to the river today because I had to see if the bottle was there with your reply.

Best wishes,
Sikander

18
A Rolltop Desk

Upstairs, at the end of the hall, beyond Gil's room, lay a small study. It was no more than eight feet square, with a single window overlooking the sea. His grandfather's office was downstairs—a large, untidy room full of books and papers. The upstairs study was completely different and felt almost empty, except for an old-fashioned, rolltop writing desk and a padded chair with rickety arms. On the floor lay a faded carpet, and against one wall stood a bookcase that was mostly empty. Only one framed picture hung in the study, an old etching of a battle scene, with soldiers and cannons. Gil didn't pay much attention to it.

He was still puzzled by the disappearance of the hand, the strange messages in the bottle, and what Lenore had told him about his future. She and Prescott had driven up to Boston that morning to attend an art exhibit. Though Gil had been invited, he had decided to stay home. Feeling bored and restless, he needed something to do. Throwing himself into the study chair, Gil tried to lift the cover of the desk but it was locked. There were drawers on either side, and when he opened the first one, he saw a tarnished brass key tied to a piece of yellow yarn. When he tried it, the key clicked smoothly in the lock and the top of the writing desk rolled up and out of sight.

Inside the desk were dozens of pigeonholes, miniature drawers and slots. It reminded Gil of a dollhouse one of his cousins used to have. The surface of the desk was covered in green felt, which had ink stains on it and was coming loose at one corner. Everything was neatly arranged inside—a set of sharpened pencils lying in a shallow groove, a couple of erasers and a copper bowl full of paper clips and pins. On one side, he saw a tiny weighing scale and an ancient-looking stapler. Each of the pigeonholes had different objects tucked inside: a pair of scissors, a magnifying glass and tweezers. Another drawer was full of used stamps and clear envelopes that looked as if they were made of waxed paper.

Exploring the desk was like exploring a house within a house, with different levels and secret compartments. Most of the things Gil found were ordinary objects: a tube of glue, a ruler, unused envelopes. But there were also unusual things: a box full of folded bits of gummed paper and a letter opener shaped like a scimitar, with a bright-colored enamel handle. In one of the upper pigeonholes, he discovered a round glass paper-weight, inside of which were swirls of orange and red that looked like flames.

The larger, lower drawers on either side of the desk were locked. Though Gil searched everywhere, he couldn't find the keys. He began to wonder whose desk this was. It couldn't have belonged to his grandmother. She and Prescott had been divorced for thirty years. Her home was in California, where she ran a strawberry farm. Maybe the desk had belonged to someone who had lived in the house before his grandfather inherited it, though some of the objects inside didn't look that old. The tube of glue was still soft, and the Magic Markers hadn't dried out. Though he knew his grandfather wouldn't care, Gil suddenly felt guilty exploring the desk, as if he were uncovering a secret identity, a mysterious presence in the house.

Moments later, he heard Kipling begin to bark downstairs. Leaving the desk, Gil went to see who it was. Kipling was standing in the main hallway, growling and snarling at the front door. There was a brass mail slot in the middle of the door, and just as Gil arrived, he saw it swing open as a letter slipped through and fell to the floor. Gil tried to make Kipling quiet down, but the dog kept barking loudly. Glancing out one of the side windows, Gil couldn't see any sign of the postman.

There was just one letter, and when he picked it up, the envelope felt heavier than he expected, the paper thick like a wedding invitation. It had an old-fashioned look about it, and there were foreign stamps, with the profile of a man in a turban. On the front was an address:

To Whom It May Concern
12 Sharia Ful Medames
Zamalek, Cairo
Egypt

This had been crossed out, and written beside it was "Please forward: P.O. Box 324, Carville, Massachusetts, USA." Stamped over this in officious black ink was "Address Unknown." There weren't any names at all, and there was no sender's address. The longer Gil held the letter, the heavier it seemed. When he flipped the envelope over, the flap was firmly glued and sealed with a circular glob of brittle red wax, at the center of which was the impression of an eight-pointed star. Though it didn't have the symbol of Mercury in the center, Gil recognized it immediately.

By this time, Kipling had quieted down, and Gil headed back upstairs to the rolltop desk. He felt an irresistible urge to open the envelope. The letter was obviously meant for someone else, yet the address was vague—"To Whom It May Concern." That could be almost anyone. Thinking about this, Gil realized he was already picking at the wax seal with his fingernail, as if it were a scab. Wondering if there was any connection between the star on the seal and the carving in the basement made him want to open the letter all the more. His fingers seemed to itch, as if every nerve in his body was prodding him to tear the envelope open.

Holding the letter up to the light, Gil tried to see what

might be inside, but the paper was much too thick. By now the envelope felt uncomfortably heavy in his hand, as if it were filled with lead.

The miniature scimitar glinted in its pigeonhole and Gil hesitantly reached across for it, taking the letter opener between his thumb and forefinger. Unable to stop himself, he slid the point of the blade under the envelope's flap. With a sudden, involuntary motion, Gil sliced it open in a single stroke.

19

The Overland Mail

"Ouch!" cries Lawrence as Tommy-two cuts off a piece of red hair with his sword.

"Hey! Stop complaining! 'Tisn't every day you get a free haircut, laddie," says Tommy-one.

The deserters have taken their hostage to an abandoned dak bungalow in the hills above Ajeebgarh. Dak bungalows are rest houses located at regular stages along highways in India, though this one happens to be situated along a road that isn't used very often. It's a damp, ruined place with spiders in the rafters, lizards on the walls, mice in the floors and snakes in the drains. The Tommies have lighted a fire, over which they roast a pigeon that one of them shot with his musket. While the deserters eat the bird, Lawrence is given a couple of moldy biscuits to chew on for dinner. When Tommy-three tosses a drumstick on the ground, Lawrence notices a scroll of paper tied to it. Cautiously, he reaches out and removes it, reading the words Sikander has written. For the first time since he's been kidnapped, Lawrence smiles.

After their meal, Tommy-one tries to write the ransom note in the firelight. He has a crumpled sheet of paper and the blunt stub of a blue pencil.

"Now, what did you say yer father's name was?" asks Tommy-one, squinting in the faint light.

"Mr. Roderick Sleeman, Esquire," says Lawrence.

Tommy-one never went to school, and the letter takes about an hour to write:

By Her Majistee's Ov'land Male
To: Mr. Rodrick Sleemin Esq.
From: Y' don't knead to kno

deer Sir,

Weev got yer son, Lawrnce. Send one
thowsind roopees kash only (Rs. 1,000) to
Peepulpatti Dak bunglo buy day aftir
tumorrow, or else wee cut ofph his head.
Don tell the powlice or miltry oficials.
(Have inclos'd as proof)

Thank'n yew sinceerlie yers kindly,
Nonymous

When the ransom note is finally written, it is folded up with the curls of red hair enclosed and stuffed into an old envelope that originally contained a notice for the three Tommies' court-martial. Finding a candle stub in the dak bungalow, Tommy-one seals the envelope with melted wax.

Though most of the mail to Ajeebgarh arrives by train, letters from the hills are delivered by overland mail carried by relays of men on foot. The next morning, soon after dawn, Lawrence hears the ringing of a bell as one of the mail runners comes down the path toward the dak bungalow. At gunpoint, Tommy-one waylays the runner and hands over the ransom note for delivery. In his broken Urdu—which is even worse than his English—he tells the mail carrier to deliver the letter to Mr. Roderick Sleeman at the Upper Finch Tea Estate. The mail runner is so frightened, he nods when asked if he understands, though he hasn't been able to comprehend a single word Tommy-one says.

Even then, the ransom note might have reached its destination, but when the mail carrier descends to the foot of the mountains, an elephant steps out of the forest and charges him. The runner drops the mail and escapes. Picking up the bag of letters with its trunk, the elephant tosses it into the trees, where a troupe of monkeys tear it open and scatter the contents. The ransom note, which could have saved Lawrence's life, ends up at the top of a banyan tree.

If only it had reached Mr. Sleeman, he would have gladly paid a thousand rupees for the release of his son. Instead, the scribbled letter gets added to a magpie's nest, a crumpled wad of paper in which two eggs are laid and later hatched.

As for Lawrence, he tries to persuade the kidnappers to let

him go, but they just laugh at him. His hands and feet are kept tied most of the time, and whenever the ropes are removed, one of the Tommies stands guard with a musket. On the third night at the dak bungalow, Lawrence is finally able to loosen the knots on his wrists. While the three deserters are snoring loudly, he slowly works his hands free, then unties his feet. Moving as silently and stealthily as he can, Lawrence crawls toward the door. His captors are sound asleep, and the only light in the room comes from the moon, which shines through a crack in the window shutters.

Getting to his feet, Lawrence can feel the prickling itch of circulation returning to his arms and legs. He reaches for the latch on the door and begins to draw it open. The rusted metal makes a grating sound, and Lawrence glances anxiously at the sleeping soldiers. One of them rolls over, making a grunting noise. Easing the latch free, he begins to push on the door. The hinges creak, but at that moment a rat comes scurrying into the room. It runs between Lawrence's feet and across the floor, scampering over the Tommies' legs.

Lawrence hears a loud curse as he rushes outdoors, no longer trying to escape quietly. Leaping from the veranda of the dak bungalow, he begins to run down the main path. Behind him, he can hear the soldiers shouting at one another and the crunch of pounding boots. In the moonlight, the forest is a confusion of shadows, and Lawrence has no idea which direction he should run.

The Tommies blunder after him as he jumps off the path and throws himself down the side of the hill, racing through the jungle and tripping over vines. The moon is mostly hidden now, except for scattered patches of light. Dense foliage encloses Lawrence in a maze of darkness. Through the treacherous night, the predators chase their prey, until at last, a musket shot rings out and all is silent . . .

20
To Whom It May Concern

Gil wasn't sure what he expected to find, but when he set aside the scimitar and unfolded the single sheet of paper, he discovered nothing more than two stanzas of poetry. From the weight of the envelope and the wax seal, he'd been imagining something much more exciting. Disappointed, Gil read the lines under his breath:

"Awake! For Morning in the Bowl of Night / Has flung the Stone that puts the Stars to Flight . . ." *Okay,* he thought. *enough! Why do poets have to use such flowery language?* But he kept on reading until he came to the second stanza: "The moving Finger writes; and having writ, / Moves on: nor all thy Piety nor Wit / Shall lure it back to cancel half a Line, / Nor all thy Tears wash out a Word of it . . ."

Boom!

Suddenly, there was a muted explosion, as if the paper Gil was holding had caught fire—a kind of spontaneous combustion. In that same moment, the ink on the page began to evaporate, the words disintegrating into a sooty cloud. Gil let go of the paper and jumped back against the wall of the study. As he watched, wide-eyed, the gray puff of smoke began to form itself into a shape, a human figure from the waist up. It was almost as if the particles of ink dust were pixels on a video screen, flickering as they rearranged themselves into a recognizable form. The words from the page had turned into a man, or at least the upper half of a man. He had no legs or feet, though he stood a few inches taller than Gil.

The clothes he wore were black and white: a formal dinner jacket with satin lapels, a starched white shirt and a striped cravat. He looked exactly like an English butler, with a thin moustache that formed two hyphens across his upper lip. His hair was slicked back from his forehead in a stylish wave.

"At your service, m'lord . . ."

"Are you talking to me?" Gil was barely able to speak.

"Naturally," said the butler with a stiff little bow. "Who else would there be?"

"I don't know," Gil stammered, "b-but who are you?"

"Aristophanes Smith, at your service. You're welcome to call me Aristo, if you wish, sir," said the butler. "I'm your personal djinn . . . or genie, as they say over here in the West. You've just let me out of my envelope."

The figure dusted off his lapels and bowed again.

"But I thought . . . ," Gil started to say, then stopped.

After an awkward pause, Aristo coughed politely. "Yes, m'lord. You were saying?"

"Aren't genies supposed to wear turbans? And have big

muscles . . . ?" Gil hesitated again, not sure if the figure would be offended.

"Well, sir. I am an English djinn. We have all sorts." The butler flexed his arms defensively. "And though I may be out of shape—having spent the last century inside an envelope—I'm sure I can lift most anything you desire."

"But I thought you came out of lamps, not envelopes . . ." This conversation was making Gil very uncomfortable.

"Another common misconception," said Aristo. "Some of us still may be found in lamps or bottles. However, letters are much more efficient and easier to dispatch."

"But I'm not sure I need a genie . . . ," said Gil.

"Well, you never know, m'lord," said Aristo with a thoughtful frown. "There's always something that needs to be done—opening locked doors, fetching groceries, making beds, doing homework, delivering messages."

"Do I get three wishes?" Gil asked cautiously.

"I'm afraid it's only two," said the genie. "Budget constraints. Unfortunately, we've had to cut back on our services."

"Okay, I'll think about it," said Gil, edging across the room toward the door.

Immediately, the genie opened it for him and said, "After you, sir."

"Um . . . listen," said Gil. "You don't need to follow me around. Maybe you could just go back into your envelope and wait until I call you."

"At your command, sir!" The genie nodded.

"Wait! That isn't one of my wishes, is it?" Gil asked quickly.

Aristo shook his head. "Only the really big ones count. You know, asking for a million dollars. Or demanding that I cut off a sultan's head."

Gil nodded. "Okay . . ."

"Right you are!" said Aristo. "I'll be here when I'm required. All you need to do is read the poem again."

Instantly, he seemed to fade away into a sprinkling of ink dust that fell back onto the sheet of paper at Gil's feet, rearranging itself into words. When he picked the poem up, Gil could see that the verses had been restored. He carefully folded the page and slid it into the envelope, which he tucked inside one of the pigeonholes in the rolltop desk. Pulling down the lid, he locked it with the brass key. After that, Gil sat down quickly to catch his breath. This time, he definitely wasn't going to tell his grandfather what he'd seen, at least not until he was absolutely sure there was a genie in the envelope.

21
Alone in the Jungle

Lawrence can smell the burnt odor of gunpowder from the musket ball that tore through the collar of his shirt, missing him by a fraction of an inch. He scrambles down the forested hillside, between huge boulders covered with moss, through narrow ravines full of rustling ferns. It is still dark but the Tommies have given up pursuit. Lawrence figures if he descends to the foot of the hill, he can find his way to Ajeebgarh by following the Magor River upstream. Tired, scraped and bruised from his escape through the jungle, he stops by a stream to drink, gulping the cool water and splashing his face. Now that dawn is approaching, he can hear all kinds of sounds in the jungle—the whistling and warbling of birds, the whooping of monkeys, even the sawing growl of a panther. But Lawrence is no longer afraid, for the thumping of the Tommies' boots has been left behind.

Heading down the stream, which he assumes will eventually flow into the river, Lawrence comes to a clearing in the valley. The ridges seem to lean backward to reveal a brightening sky. The moon has set and most of the stars have disappeared, but just above the treetops, Lawrence can see a tiny pinprick of light, its edges blurred, but shining with a persistence that seems to defy the dawn.

"Mercury," Lawrence whispers to himself. Last year, his mother taught him the names of the planets as they sat on the lawns of the planter's bungalow, gazing up at the night sky. "Mercury, the messenger," his mother had explained. The memory of her voice, describing the stars and constellations, makes him feel suddenly helpless and alone. As his eyes fill with tears, the planet seems to melt away.

Shaking off his emotions, Lawrence continues along the streambed, moving as quickly as he can in the half-light. By the time he is out of the mountains, the sun is already high overhead and the air is hot and humid. Swarms of mosquitoes and gnats hum about his ears, and Lawrence wishes it was dark and cool again. He begins to wonder if the stream will actually lead him to the river. It seems to go on and on. Now that he is on the plains, his sense of direction becomes confused. For three days, all he has eaten are a couple of moldy biscuits. Hunger and exhaustion make him delirious. He thinks he sees a mango tree full of ripe fruit, but when he tries to climb it, the branches are covered with thorns. The round white rocks in the streambed look like melons, but when Lawrence reaches down to pick one up, imagining the sweet juice dribbling down his chin, the stone is burning hot from the sun and as heavy as an iron cannonball.

Stumbling now, barely able to walk, he sees what looks like the mast of a sailing ship, with some kind of rigging. Lawrence raises one hand, as if he were a castaway on a desert island, and begins to run toward the ship with its tall, straight mast. He trips, then gets to his feet again, finally throwing himself against the wooden post. In his muddled mind, he realizes this isn't a ship, but something much better—a telegraph pole. Wiping the stinging sweat from his eyes, he can see the copper wires leading straight through the jungle to Ajeebgarh. Fifty yards ahead is another pole, and another one after that.

Crawling to the stream, he takes a drink of water, though it makes his empty stomach turn. Looking up to see the telegraph pole again, his vision is blurred and he blinks his eyes. In front of him is a wavering line, like a swaying mirage. Is it a hand, waving at him? A rope dangling in the air? He blinks again. This time when he opens his eyes, Lawrence sees a king cobra. The snake's hood is unfurled, and it is prepared to strike.

22
The Philatelist

That afternoon, Gil walked over to Nargis's house as soon as she got home from school. When he told her about the genie, she didn't seem convinced, but he offered to prove it to her. Together they headed back to the Yankee Mahal. When they went upstairs to the study, Prescott was sitting at the rolltop desk, leaning over a thick album, with a magnifying glass in one hand.

"Grandpa, what are you doing here?" asked Gil.

Prescott gave him a sheepish smile. "Nothing much," he said. "Just a hobby of mine."

"It's a stamp collection," said Nargis.

Prescott nodded as Gil made sure the letter he had opened earlier was still in its pigeonhole.

"Can we have a look?" Nargis asked.

"Sure, if you really want to," said Prescott. "Most people find stamp collecting boring, but I've been a philatelist since I was eight years old."

As Gil and Nargis leaned over to look at the album, they saw a dozen two-cent stamps displayed on the page, all of them with George Washington's face. Each one looked exactly the same.

"I just got this stamp today," said Prescott, pointing to one at the bottom, "from a dealer in Virginia. I've been negotiating with him for a couple of weeks and he finally lowered the price."

"How much did it cost?" asked Gil.

His grandfather winced with embarrassment. "A hundred and twenty dollars," he said.

"What? Are you kidding?" said Gil with a laugh. "That's a two-cent stamp."

"It must be pretty rare," said Nargis.

Prescott nodded. "It's from 1848. I've been trying to find one of these for years, to complete my collection. You see, each one is different." Taking the magnifying glass, he ran it over the stamps, pointing out the slight variations in printing and color. One of the stamps had George Washington facing in the opposite direction.

"That's the rarest one of all," said Prescott, "because it's reversed."

"How much is it worth?" said Gil.

"A thousand dollars at least."

"Whoa!" Nargis whispered.

Prescott turned the page and showed them a set of stamps with Alexander Hamilton's face on them. Another page had nothing but Benjamin Franklin. Even though they were worth a lot of money, Gil couldn't understand why anyone would get excited by stamps with pictures of dead patriots and presidents.

"Let me show you the first collection I ever made," said Prescott, unlocking one of the lower drawers of the desk. He took out a smaller, scuffed album with a leather cover and thick black pages. The album contained more than two hundred stamps from America and other countries like Mexico, France and England.

"When I started, I collected everything I could find and stuck them in this album in random order. Later, I started to get more specialized. Now I collect mostly nineteenth-century American stamps."

Gil flipped through the pages of Prescott's first album, which had descriptions and dates written in white ink on the black pages. The handwriting was childish but neat.

"Every stamp is a story," his grandfather said. "You see that one with the yellow butterfly? It's from Vietnam, or Indochine, as it used to be called under the French. When I was still in seventh grade, back in 1953, my father got a letter from a man in Saigon. I soaked the stamp off the envelope and added it to my collection. Whenever I see that butterfly, I think of that day, and how naive I was. I'd never heard of Vietnam before. A few years later, it was a place we'd never forget. A lot of my friends were fighting over there, and I was in jail as a conscientious objector."

"What's that?" asked Gil.

"A pacifist," said Prescott. "I refused to be drafted and join the army."

This was something else Gil had never known about his grandfather. For a moment, he forgot about the stamps.

"How long were you in jail?" he asked, intrigued.

"Six months," Prescott replied. "After that I did Alternative Service, teaching at a school for the blind in Alabama. It was the most important experience of my life, teaching Shakespeare in Braille."

"What's in the other albums?" Nargis asked.

"Mostly American stamps. These are from an earlier period." Gil could see that the dates were printed on the outside of each album. 1870–1879. 1880–1889. Unlocking a second drawer, Prescott took out an album embossed with ornate gold patterns.

"Here's one that might interest you," he said. "I've got a complete collection of stamps from the kingdom of Ajeebgarh, which no longer exists. It's part of India now. The maharajah issued his own postage until the British forced him to stop. I got interested in Ajeebgarh because that was where Ezekiel Finch had his tea estates. He died there in 1879. Among our family papers we had a lot of his old letters that carried these stamps and I've been able to put together a complete collection."

Nargis nudged Gil with her elbow and the two of them exchanged startled glances. Most of the stamps in the album had pictures of the maharajah on them. Gil recognized his profile from the postage on the genie's envelope.

"Maharajah Lajawab Singh II," said Prescott. "He was an interesting man, who wanted to turn his kingdom into a modern state. The post and telegraph office in Ajeebgarh was one of the most efficient in India. Lajawab Singh II had all sorts of trouble with the British, who thought he was an upstart, full of dangerous ideas. He insisted on issuing his own postage and brought the telegraph to Ajeebgarh. Supposedly, Lajawab Singh was also negotiating with the Russians to export his tea. Eventually the British invaded Ajeebgarh and took over the kingdom by force. It's sometimes referred to as the Postage Stamp War."

Staring down at the page full of stamps, Gil could barely contain his excitement. When he looked across at Nargis, he could tell she too was thinking about Sikander.

Prescott stopped himself for a moment and pointed to the picture on the wall, an etching of a battle scene.

"Here you go," he said. "I found this in an antiques shop a couple years back. It's a picture from the *London Illustrated News* that shows the siege of Ajeebgarh. This was printed in 1896. You can see the maharajah's palace in ruins."

Gil and Nargis squinted at the old print, which showed a lot of British officers waving their swords about and cannons spewing clouds of smoke. One of the maharajah's soldiers was trying to fight back, but he was wounded and had fallen to one knee. Reminded of Sikander again, Gil shuddered and wondered if he was all right.

Picking up the magnifying glass, he studied the jewels on the maharajah's turban and the way his moustache curled up at the ends. It was definitely the same man pictured on the stamp on the genie's envelope. Hesitating, Gil reached for the letter.

"Grandpa . . . ," he said, "I found this today."

Prescott took it from him, ignoring the address and training the magnifying lens on the stamp instead.

"Look at that!" he said with excitement. "It says 1896. The

117

cancellation mark is smudged, but you can tell by the sash he's wearing. Where did you get this?" Prescott fixed his eyes on Gil.

"Um . . . this morning, it arrived through the mail slot while you were away . . ."

His grandfather stared at him suspiciously, then turned back to examine the stamps.

"Actually . . . ," said Gil, swallowing hard. "There's something inside the envelope you might want to see."

Prescott still looked confused. He opened the paper, flattening it on the green baize surface of the desk.

"What's this?" he said with an interested frown, recognizing the verses. *The Rubaiyat of Omar Khayyam.* He began to read the lines: "'Awake! for Morning in the bowl of Night / Has flung the Stone that puts the Stars to Flight . . .'"

Gil waited for something to happen but there wasn't any explosion or puff of smoke. When Prescott finished reading the poem, he shook his head and smiled, then went back to examining the stamp. No genie had appeared, and Gil exchanged a puzzled glance with Nargis. He took the letter and held it up to the light. The ink remained fixed to the page.

23

Salvilinus frontinalis

Ezekiel Finch kneels beside the slate-lined tank and watches the tiny fingerlings swarming through the clear, cold water. The sight of their tapered bodies wriggling against the gentle current fills him with a feeling of satisfaction and regret.

Late last year, on a bright November day, before he sailed from Hornswoggle Bay, Ezekiel had cast his fly line into the ice pond near his house. A fat brook trout took the fly and he played her into shore. She was full of roe, and when he held her over a basin and squeezed her belly, the eggs had squirted out like seeds from an overripe tomato. After collecting these, he released the fish back into the pond and cast again. The autumn colors in the trees were as full of gold as a pharaoh's tomb. Within an hour, Ezekiel had landed twelve trout, most of which were ready to spawn. Finally, he had hooked a male brook trout that leapt on the surface of the pond, in a fierce struggle to throw the hook. Holding the line firmly, Ezekiel drew the fish to shore. The male trout was smaller than the others, a bright orange and mottled green, its spawning colors as gaudy as the maple leaves. In the basin, hundreds of clear trout ova were mixed with white milt from the male, just as they might have been fertilized in the pebbled shallows of the pond.

Later, the eggs were transferred into three glass jars, full of water and gravel, which were taken aboard the *Moorish Queen*. Throughout the long voyage to India, Ezekiel had the water siphoned out and replaced each day to keep the eggs alive. Ezekiel himself had turned his back on New England, with a sad, stern look on his face. He was a hardy, self-made man, not given to outward emotions, but as he sailed beyond the headland and caught a last glimpse of the high slate roof of the Yankee Mahal, his eyes glistened with remorse.

Stone by stone, he had built that house, dreaming of carrying Camellia over the threshold one day. It was to be a home in which they raised a family and lived in contentment for the rest of their lives. But the dream had frozen over as quickly as the surface of the ice pond in December. Ezekiel had nothing left to live for there. His ships, with their cargo of tea and ice, had made him a wealthy man, but none of that mattered, now that Camellia had refused to give him her hand in marriage.

The only thing Ezekiel took with him from Massachusetts, to remind him of bright autumn days like this, was the brood of fish eggs. In the foothills of the eastern Himalayas above Ajeebgarh, he planned to stock a pond with trout. Everything else he left behind, his house with all its furnishings, his horses, his orchards, his land. Never again would he see the foliage turn gold in autumn, or feel the crunch of snow beneath his boots, or touch Camellia's soft brown hair. Instead, he sailed away to a lonely exile in the East.

And now, as he kneels beside his fish hatchery, watching the fingerlings swimming back and forth, he realizes how far he's come. Ambital is no bigger than the ice pond—a secluded lake in the mountains above the tea estates he owns. Unlike the European brown trout (*Salmo trutta*), brought by the British to other parts of India, these American brook trout are a different species—*Salvilinus frontinalis*. Ezekiel will release the fish halfway around the globe, as a tragic reminder of his loss and a wriggling testament of thwarted hopes.

24
Beyond Xanadu

Leaving Prescott to his stamp collection, Gil and Nargis took the poem and went out to the garage. Leaning against Prescott's Volkswagen, Gil shook his head.

"I swear, the last time I read this poem, a genie appeared. I can't figure out why it didn't work."

Nargis took the paper from his hands and began to read the verses aloud. As soon as she reached the last line, there was a muted explosion and the ink disintegrated into a whirligig of smoke. Dropping the paper, Nargis jumped back, almost tripping over a lawn mower.

"At your service m'lord!" said the genie.

Gil swallowed hard. "Why didn't you appear when my grandfather read the poem?"

The genie shrugged. "I was off duty," he explained. "Elevenses."

Nargis stared at the apparition that hovered inside the garage, like a cloud with a human face.

"What do you mean?" said Gil. "I thought you were supposed to be here whenever I need you."

The genie took a pocket watch out of his waistcoat and wound the knob.

"Well, that's true, sir. But we genies operate on a strict schedule, negotiated and agreed upon by common consent. You see, I break for breakfast from eight to nine, then elevenses at eleven o'clock, of course. Lunch is from half past noon to two o'clock. Afternoon tea: three to four thirty. Dinner is six to nine PM. After that I'm off until seven AM."

"That doesn't leave you much time to work," said Gil.

"We also get Saturdays and Sundays off, as well as bank holidays," said Aristo, polishing his watch and returning it to his pocket.

Nargis didn't like the genie much. After the first shock of seeing him rise up off the page, she found him pompous and condescending. Though he greeted Nargis with formality and called her "m'lady," he seemed much more interested in talking with Gil, as if girls were a waste of his time. He had an annoying way of sniffing when he spoke, and his hands were always making dismissive gestures in her direction. For all his mysteriousness and magic, Nargis could tell that Aristophanes Smith was a very ordinary genie who liked to put on airs.

Before going back into his envelope, he insisted on reciting "Kubla Khan" by Samuel Taylor Coleridge.

In Xanadu did Kubla Khan
A stately pleasure-dome decree:

Where Alph, the sacred river, ran
Through caverns measureless to man
Down to a sunless sea.
So twice five miles of fertile ground
With walls and towers were girdled round:
And there were gardens bright with sinuous rills
Where blossom'd many an incense-bearing tree;
And here were forests ancient as the hills,
Enfolding sunny spots of greenery . . .

The first part of the poem was all right, but after that it got long-winded as Aristo droned on until the end. While reciting the poem, he tucked one hand between the buttons of his waistcoat and the other he waved about like an orchestra conductor. During this performance Nargis nudged Gil's arm and rolled her eyes.

After the poem was finished, Gil nodded, then asked Aristo to explain how he'd got into the envelope in the first place.

"With the help of a calligrapher's pen," said the genie. "Naturally—or supernaturally as the case may be—there are certain things I can't reveal, but suffice it to say that my existence depends upon a process of versification and reversification, if you know what I mean."

"No, I don't," said Gil.

"Well, sir. Since your grandfather is a poet, I would imagine you understand the power of language and metaphor . . ."

Gil shrugged.

"And you're familiar with the literary theory of relative cor-relatives?"

"No . . ."

"It's really nothing more than that . . ."—Aristo flicked his wrist— "along with a few secret ingredients in the calligra-pher's ink. You could say I'm the soul of the poem, the spirit of the words rising up off the page. Omar Khayyam's lyrics are translated into English and therefore, ergo, I am an English ge-nie. If the *Rubaiyat*'s quatrains had been written in the original Farsi, I would have been a Persian genie. We can be translated into any language you like—except Latin or Sanskrit, which have been recently discontinued."

"The envelope was addressed to Cairo," said Gil. "Was that where you were supposed to go?"

"Indeed. My original assignment was to serve an eminent Egyptologist, who was trying to uncover the secrets of Queen Hetshepsut's tomb. I was sent to help him decipher the hiero-glyphics, but he was caught smuggling mummies out of the country and had to leave abruptly, before my letter arrived."

"What happened after that?" asked Nargis.

"Well, I kicked around Cairo for a while—nice city but dif-ficult to enjoy if you're trapped inside an envelope. Eventually, someone sent me off to a nonexistent postbox, here in Massa-chusetts. It was a false address the Egyptologist used, to keep the authorities off his trail."

"And then?" said Nargis impatiently. Aristo looked at her in disdain, polishing his fingernails on his lapel.

"Well, that was it!" he said. "I was trapped inside a dead letter. Address Unknown. End of the road."

"But how did you get delivered here?" Gil asked.

"Oh, that?" he said. "It's a secret."

"Come on!" said Nargis. "You can't tell us this whole elaborate story, then keep the end to yourself. I don't believe a word of what you've said."

The genie looked at Gil as if expecting help, but Gil shook his head.

"All right . . . ," said the genie at last. "But this has got to be between us. Super-confidential. Top secret. For your ears only."

"Go on," said Nargis.

"I was delivered by hand . . . ," whispered the genie.

"Whose hand?" said Gil.

The genie shuddered.

"A rather revolting hand, if you ask me," he replied, still under his breath. "A bony, shriveled hand without any skin or flesh. Just a skeletal hand on its own, with an absolutely nauseating smell."

25

Penmanship

November 11. Veterans Day. Gil was surprised when his grandfather suggested they go to the parade in Carville.

"I thought you were a pacifist," said Gil.

"Sure," said Prescott. "But that doesn't mean I can't go and watch the parade. A lot of my friends are veterans, or were . . ."

At nine thirty that morning, Lenore came across to join them and they drove down and parked near the town hall. It was an overcast, blustery day, and the parade didn't take more than half an hour. There were a couple of Humvees from the National Guard and a line of antique cars full of men in old uniforms with medals on their chests. Some of the veterans drove past on motorcycles and the crowd clapped and cheered. Three men in colonial uniforms played "Yankee Doodle" on drums and pipes. The Stars and Stripes was raised over the town green, and everyone sang the national anthem. Nargis and her parents had also come to watch the parade.

Afterward, she joined Gil as he walked across to the cemetery, along with Prescott and Lenore. At the gate of the cemetery was a memorial to all of the soldiers from Hornswoggle Bay who had died in the Civil War. Someone had put a red, white and blue wreath in front of it.

First they went to visit Lenore's grandfather's grave. He had fought in World War I and was wounded in Italy. His tomb lay on one of the upper terraces, and Lenore placed a bunch of flowers against the stone. There was already a miniature flag planted in the ground. After that they visited the graves of Prescott's uncles, who had been soldiers in World War II and Korea. They were buried a short ways down the hill in a family plot. There was also a cousin of Prescott's who had died in Vietnam. All three had flags next to their headstones. Seeing the name *Finch* carved in granite gave Gil a strange feeling, even though he hadn't known any of these relatives. Looking across the cemetery, he could see hundreds of other flags fluttering in the breeze. It seemed as if almost every second grave marked the final resting place of a soldier or sailor.

"Come on," said Lenore, after they'd finished paying their respects. "I'll show you something."

Picking their way between the graves, they followed Lenore across to a large chestnut tree. Here the stones were older, many of them thin slabs of slate with the lettering worn and weathered like the inscriptions in the basement of the Yankee Mahal. Near the roots of the chestnut lay a simple granite marker.

CAMELLIA STUBBS

September 3, 1812—April 20, 1912

For a minute or two nobody said anything. Lenore leaned down and brushed a couple of dead leaves off the stone.

"Isn't she the woman who was supposed to marry Ezekiel Finch?" Gil asked.

Prescott nodded. "That's her."

"She lived to be nearly a hundred," said Nargis softly.

"Camellia Stubbs was a schoolmistress," said Lenore. "She never married. A spinster all her life. For years, almost everybody in this town was a student of hers. Camellia was well loved but very strict. She insisted that all of her students practice perfect penmanship. If anyone's handwriting was messy, she would snatch the paper off their desks and crumple it up. Even now, they say her hand crawls out of her casket and goes from house to house, searching through papers and letters. When she doesn't like the penmanship on a page, the fingers crumple up the sheet of paper and throw it in the wastebasket—just as the schoolmistress used to do with her students' writing."

◆   ◆   ◆

After visiting the cemetery, they all drove back to the Yankee Mahal, where Lenore put water on for tea.

"There are dozens of ways to make tea," she said, "but when I was living in England, years ago, I was taught the proper method . . . First you warm the pot like this . . ." She opened the lid of a white porcelain teapot and poured in a cupful of boiling water, swishing it around for a moment, then emptying it in the sink. Nargis and Gil watched as she took a packet of tea leaves and added four generous pinches.

"One for each of us, and one for the pot," she said. Prescott was sitting at the kitchen table with Kipling at his feet.

"Am I not included?" he asked.

Lenore gave him an impatient smile. "No," she said. "You can stick to your iced tea."

The kettle on the stove was still boiling, sending out a plume of steam.

"Bubble bubble, toil and trouble, cauldron boil and . . . ," Prescott teased her. "There's witchcraft in making tea."

"The secret is really in the water," Lenore continued, ignoring Prescott. "You have to make sure it's fresh—no chlorine or minerals to spoil the taste."

She poured the boiling water into the pot, put on the lid and covered it with a quilted tea cozy.

"Why don't you use tea bags?" Gil asked.

Lenore gave him a disapproving look. "It's not the same as loose tea," she said. "Doesn't have the same flavor."

Gil picked up the packet and read the blue label, which had a picture of a tea picker on it.

FLOWERY ORANGE PEKOE

Superlative Whole Leaf Tea

UPPER FINCH ESTATE

Ajeebgarh

India

"Hey, is this from . . . ?" He turned to look at his grandfather, who nodded.

"Yes it is," said Prescott. "That tea is grown in the same gardens that Ezekiel Finch once owned."

Gil ran his fingers through the dark, brittle leaves, then sniffed at the packet, which had a rich aroma.

"Ajeebgarh tea is a lot like Darjeeling, which grows forty miles to the east. Some people claim it's the best tea in the world," said Prescott.

"I've tried all kinds of tea, from Ceylon, China, Assam and Kenya," Lenore added. "But Ajeebgarh tea has a special taste and color. You have to be patient and let the tea steep for a full five minutes. Timing is crucial. If you drink it too quickly, you don't get the full zest. Let it sit too long and it grows bitter."

Gil and Nargis helped take cups and saucers down from the cupboard. Lenore had brought a plate of freshly baked chocolate chip cookies, which lay on the counter.

"You can offer your grandfather one of these," she said, winking at Gil. "And help yourselves too."

Each of them ate a cookie while they waited for the tea. Prescott broke his in half and slipped part of it to the dog, who immediately got up to beg for more.

Lenore glanced at her watch, then removed the tea cozy and opened the pot, sniffing the fragrance with an appreciative nod.

"Now, most people strain their tea," said Lenore. "But we're going to let the leaves settle in your cup."

After their cups had been filled, Lenore added a spoon of sugar to each and handed them around. Holding the cups and saucers, Gil and Nargis looked at each other self-consciously, as if they were expected to sip politely.

When they finished their tea, Lenore closed her eyes for a moment, savoring the aftertaste. Then she leaned over each cup, studying the dregs at the bottom. The shriveled black leaves had opened up in the boiling water and now lay unfurled. After the ritual of making and serving the tea, it felt as if something important was going to happen. Even Prescott had fallen silent, watching Lenore.

"What do you see?" Nargis asked.

"Something of the past," said Lenore, her voice softer and deeper than before. "Something of the present. And something of the future."

The three white cups sat before her like newly hatched eggs. Lenore turned to Gil with a curious expression.

"Do you remember what I told you the other day," she asked, "when I read your palm?"

Gil nodded.

"It's true," she said with a reassuring smile. "I can see it in the leaves. Everything is written here just as it was on your hand and in the stars. What did I say?"

Gil looked across at his grandfather nervously. "You said I was going to be a messenger of peace."

"And . . . ?" Lenore urged him on.

"One day I'd save someone's life." Gil didn't dare look at Nargis.

"What about love?" said Lenore.

Gil felt himself blushing. He shook his head.

"Come on," Lenore prompted. "Didn't I say, 'You hold the key of love in your heart'?"

"I guess," Gil admitted.

"It's all true," Lenore said. "Tea leaves never lie."

Nargis wanted to laugh but controlled herself for Gil's sake. After a moment she got up the courage to speak.

"What about the past?" she asked. "You said you could read the past and present in the tea leaves too."

"Of course." Lenore nodded. "But today it's all one and the same. Whatever happens in the present or the future will affect the past."

Gil stared down at Kipling, who was curled up at his feet. He knew that everyone else had their eyes on him, and he wondered how he could possibly do what Lenore had predicted—be a messenger of peace, save a life, or hold the key of love in his heart. It sounded like one of those cheesy messages in a birthday card. Even if he could . . . did he really want to do any of those things?

26
The Himalayan Mail

From the roof of his house, Sikander can see the railway tracks leading to Ajeebgarh Station. Once a week, every Thursday evening, he listens for the whistle of the *Himalayan Mail* that travels all the way across India, from Bombay. The train carries passengers and freight, but its most important cargo are the letters delivered from around the world. Whenever Sikander sees the silvery line of parallel tracks, running through the outskirts of the town and leading into the fields and forests beyond, he can almost hear the far-off rumble of the wheels and the breathless panting of the steam engine.

The *Himalayan Mail* usually arrives at dusk. First there is the whistle as it passes over a bridge across the Magor River, then puffs of smoke against the twilight sky. Finally, the engine comes into view, its headlamp burning as darkness settles. Sikander strains his eyes to see the carriages that follow, their segmented shapes crawling toward Ajeebgarh. As the train comes closer, he can see the glowing cinders blowing out of the locomotive's smokestack, and the burning embers of coal falling onto the tracks. As the *Himalayan Mail* passes his house, Sikander watches the huge wheels pumping forward, as if straining to reach their destination. The clamor of steel and steam drowns out all other noises as the engine throbs and rattles, thunders and wheezes. Once again the whistle blows. Mixed with the black smoke are white plumes of steam. Sikander wonders what kind of ink he could make out of the soot from this engine. Overnight, the *Himalayan Mail* halts in Ajeebgarh, and leaves the next morning at dawn. Sikander gets up to watch it depart, every Friday morning, as the sky brightens. At six o'clock the whistle sounds more strident, as if the train were impatient to be on its way, carrying sacks of mail, as well as shipments of tea in the goods wagons and travelers in their first-, second- and third-class carriages. Sikander can see the driver leaning out of his cabin, and stokers shoveling coal into the fiery mouth of the engine. Occasionally, the train is late, but the *Himalayan Mail* always arrives and departs along the same straight line of rails, carrying its freight of words.

Though Sikander cannot see him, a passenger is seated alone in a first-class compartment. He wears a coat and scarf, and on the berth beside him lies a dented felt hat. This man glances out the window and sees the rooftops of Ajeebgarh silhouetted against the sunrise. He checks his watch, then pulls the shutter down and locks the door. From under his seat, where the porters stowed his luggage, the man takes out a typewriter case and places it on a folding table next to the window. Opening the case, he touches the keys softly, as if he were a pianist testing to see if his instrument is tuned.

The first-class passenger then takes a sheet of paper and rolls it into the typewriter, pausing for a moment to collect his thoughts. He begins to type with one finger, a single letter at a time. The steady clicking of the typewriter echoes the rattle of the wheels. At the end of each line, the passenger slides the lever and the roller moves across, like the train in which he travels, a journey of words shuttling back and forth upon the page.

When the conductor raps on the door to check his ticket, the passenger carefully closes the typewriter case before unfastening the latch. After his ticket has been canceled, he locks the door again. His face is pale, though his hair and moustache are as black as the sleek silk ribbon of the typewriter. Before removing the sheet of paper, he reads over what he has written:

ZGH LTEKTZ

O IQCT DTZ VOZI COSSQFGC. IT QLLXKTL DT

KXLLOQ IQL FG OFZTKTLZ OF QPTTWUQKI ZTQ.

FG FTTR ZG RTESQKT VQK.

KTUQKRL, ITKDTL

With a satisfied nod, the passenger folds the paper into a square, then slips it into an envelope. Hesitating for a moment, he peels the false moustache off his upper lip and tucks it between the folds of the letter, before sealing it up.

27
Parcel Post

At the corner of Forsythia Lane and Oswald Street, Nargis could see the winking red lights on the postman's jeep. It was parked where it always was, between the DEAD END sign and the fire hydrant. The postman usually did his rounds at the same time Nargis got home from school. Turning into Forsythia Lane, she could see him stuffing letters into a neighbor's mailbox. Pedaling as fast as she could, Nargis skidded to a stop in her driveway just as Mr. Griswold arrived at the house.

"Hey there!" he said.

"Hi, Mr. Griswold," said Nargis. "Any letters for me?"

"Let's have a look," said the postman, searching through his bag. First he took out a bundle of mail wrapped with a rubber band. Then he found a couple of flyers from the supermarket. After that he pulled out a package covered in brown paper and tied up with string.

"Nothing for you," he said. "But here's a parcel for your mother. Will you sign for it?"

Nargis took the pen he gave her and scrawled her name on the receipt. With her book bag from school and her hands full of mail, it was difficult to unlock the front door. When she got inside, Nargis dumped everything on the dining table. Her mother wouldn't be home from work for another hour at least, and her father usually didn't get back until after dark.

The parcel had been sent from India. Nargis could tell it was from her aunt in Delhi, her mother's younger sister. Though it wasn't very heavy, the package was as bulky as one of the cushions on the sofa. The brown paper had torn at a couple of places and Nargis could see plastic wrapping inside, but not enough to reveal the contents. The twine that held it together made her think something inside was going to pop open as soon as the knots were untied. She couldn't imagine what the parcel contained. Maybe clothes? A sweater? (Her aunt was always knitting.) Something to eat? Nargis sniffed the package but it didn't have much of a smell, only a dusty odor of paper and plastic.

More than a dozen stamps were stuck together in one corner of the parcel like an untidy mosaic. One of them had a picture of a red panda feeding on bamboo. Nargis knew that her aunt loved wildlife and always chose stamps with animals. There were two rhinos, six tigers and a couple of peacocks all glued together on the parcel and canceled in black ink. The patchwork of postage added up to more than two hundred rupees. Nargis studied the stamps as if they might be clues to what lay inside. She shook the package to see if it contained anything that made a sound. Nargis knew she had to wait until her mother got home. Shuffling through the rest of the mail, she found nothing but bills and credit card offers.

To distract herself, Nargis switched on the TV, but there wasn't anything worth watching, just a couple of old sitcoms she'd seen before. Even the nature programs weren't interesting—the life cycle of tent worms. Switching channels, Nargis kept going back to the parcel, pinching it gently and weighing it in one hand.

Finally, she took her book bag upstairs and sat down to do her homework. The only assignment Nargis had was to write a book report on a novel she'd just read. Nargis sat down at her desk and started writing in her notebook. Her teacher had asked only for a rough draft of the book report. Nargis wrote as quickly as she could, knowing that later she would copy it over neatly. The more she wrote, the sloppier her handwriting became.

Most of the notebook page was full when she heard her mother's car pull into the driveway. As soon as Savita Khanna came through the kitchen door, Nargis stood in front of her, holding the parcel in both hands.

"Open it," she demanded.

Her mother didn't seem to be in any hurry and laughed as Nargis followed her around with the package. After leaving her bags in the kitchen, then checking the messages on the answering machine and putting a kettle on for tea, Nargis's mother finally got a pair of scissors and cut the twine. The parcel looked like a huge cocoon, and Nargis almost expected a giant butterfly or moth to burst through the wrapping and open its wings.

"Do you know what it is?" Nargis asked.

Her mother nodded, giving nothing away. She began to peel off the tape, slowly, deliberately. Nargis wanted to claw at the parcel and rip it open. It seemed as if her mother was torturing her on purpose by taking so long. Under the layers of paper and plastic was another bag. Eventually, when this was opened, Mrs. Khanna took out a folded bundle of purple fabric. Nargis sat down in disappointment.

"It's only a sari," she said, making a face.

"What did you expect?" her mother asked.

"I don't know," said Nargis. "Something exciting."

"But look at the silk," her mother said. "And the embroidery. It's beautiful, isn't it?"

Nargis shrugged. Her mother wore saris only on special occasions, if there was a wedding, or on festivals like Diwali when they got together with other Indian families.

As her mother turned the cloth over in her hands, the light caught the changing colors in the silk—an iridescent hue. Nargis shifted onto the sofa next to her mother and ran her fingers over the sari. The folds of silk flowed against each other as if the layers of fabric were fluid. Though Nargis wore only jeans and sweatshirts, there was something about the sari that intrigued her. She touched the gold embroidery along the hem, a delicate pattern of gilded threads that formed a paisley design. At one end of the sari was a wide border of embroidery.

"This is the pallav," said her mother. "It goes over your shoulder."

"How long is a sari?" Nargis asked as the fabric spilled over her knees and onto the carpet.

"Six yards," her mother explained. "Most of it gets pleated at your waist."

"When did you learn to tie a sari?" Nargis asked.

"I was about your age," said Savita Khanna. "But I didn't wear one until much later."

"It must be hard to tie," said Nargis.

"Not really," her mother said. "Here, I'll show you."

Nargis stood up as her mother wrapped one end around her waist. She had to hitch it up so the fabric didn't drag on the ground. Quickly, with expert hands, Mrs. Khanna wound the purple silk around her daughter's faded jeans, then pleated it together between her fingers until it fell in a neat cascade. Tucking the sari in at the waist, she smoothed out the places where the sweatshirt had bunched up. Nargis felt as if she were being gift wrapped. Looking down, she could see the shimmering colors in the silk. After this, her mother took the loose end of the sari, with the embroidered pallav, and draped it over Nargis's shoulder. At first, Nargis was afraid to walk. Her mother laughed as she shuffled forward with baby steps to look at herself in the mirror in the downstairs bathroom. She was sure she was going to trip over the sari, though the sound of rustling silk made her feel as if she were gliding across the hardwood floor.

When she switched on the bathroom light and looked in

the mirror, Nargis hardly recognized herself. The yards of purple silk made her look more elegant than she had ever felt before, like a princess or a movie star.

"Don't admire yourself too much," Mrs. Khanna teased.

After unwinding the sari with her mother's help, Nargis headed up to her room to finish her book report. Opening the door, she went across to her desk, then stopped . . .

The book report was gone! The page had been torn out of her notebook. When she glanced around, Nargis saw it crumpled up and lying in the wastebasket. Folding her arms to keep from shaking, she recognized a bad smell in the room, a combination of spoiled milk and lilac perfume.

28
First Snow

Next morning Gil woke up earlier than usual, about six thirty. The first smudge of daylight shone through the windowpanes and the radiator was hissing and clicking. It had suddenly turned cold. When he looked out the window, he was surprised to see it was snowing. Flakes were coming down lightly and the lawn outside was dusted white. Thirsty, Gil went downstairs to the kitchen, crossing through the unlighted rooms of the Yankee Mahal. After filling a glass with water, he headed back to bed. On the way, he noticed a light in his grandfather's study and the door was open a crack. He wondered if Prescott was awake.

Tapping softly, Gil listened but there was no response. Cautiously, he pushed the door open and saw that the desk lamp was on beside the typewriter. Papers and books were everywhere, stacked on the floor, stuffed into shelves, propped against the windowsill. His grandfather wasn't in his chair.

Gil took a couple of steps into the room and saw a piece of paper next to the typewriter with a poem written on it. He hadn't read any of his grandfather's books. His parents had never encouraged him to do so. But the title of the poem caught his eye.

OLD DOG

Gil knew it had to be about Kipling, and when he picked the paper up, he scanned the typed lines. Some words were crossed out with blue ink, and there were phrases inserted in the margins.

All that's left for him in life is smell and taste,
his other senses dulled . . .
Eyes gone milky, ears deaf to my commands.
But odors still excite him. Make him young again.
The old dog inhales a whiff of fish guts,
the scent of raccoons around the garbage cans,
loves nothing more than to revel in a smell—
rotten blue jay's egg . . . skunk scat—
as if to mask his own canine fragrances.
It's the bloodhound in him more than setter,
an olfactory pedigree.
Luxuriating in the stench of decadence,
the bouquet of goose dung,
aroma of moldy cheddar.
Eau de toilet.

He's redolent with age
Proud of his pungent colognes.

(They say dogs read with their noses,
finding poetry in the soil.)

Gil recognized his grandfather's voice in the words, the rambling drawl of their conversations at the kitchen table. As he put the paper down, there was a sound behind him, the door creaking open. Gil spun around as a black nose and white muzzle poked through the shadows.

"Kip!" he said, exhaling with relief. "You scared me."

The dog stumbled into the room and put his nose in Gil's hand, licking his fingers. With a last glimpse back at the desk, Gil turned and led the old dog to his room. Kip had some trouble climbing the stairs, his hind legs stiff with arthritis.

Later that morning, after his grandfather was awake and making breakfast, Gil took Kipling outside in the backyard and let him sniff around the house. The snow was still falling lightly, powdering the dry leaves with a coat of white. Kip still hadn't been fed, so he wasn't likely to run away, though he seemed friskier than usual and even chased a squirrel that tried to sneak past him from the garage to the hickory trees at the back. A little later, he found an old tennis ball and brought it to Gil, wagging his tail. Though he could hardly see, Kipling still liked to chase a ball. Gil threw it close by and the dog raced after the ball, snuffling about in the grass to see where it had gone.

All at once, Kipling stopped, as if he'd been brought up

short by an invisible leash. With his tail rigid and one forepaw raised, he stood there pointing at an empty flower bed, where Prescott had been planting crocus bulbs the day before. Gil felt the hairs on his arms begin to rise and he held back for a moment. Going forward cautiously, he looked about in the direction where Kipling was pointing. The tennis ball lay unretrieved and there was nothing else around, except for a trowel, which was covered with a sprinkling of snow. Gil's eyes traced every inch of ground until he caught his breath.

There in the white layer of snow upon the flower bed, he could see fresh footprints. But unlike the ridged pattern of his grandfather's gardening boots or the worn-down tread of his own sneakers, these footprints were completely smooth. The strange part was that the footprints hadn't been there a few seconds ago, and almost immediately they began to disappear. The marks were outlined with a faint dusting of ash.

29

The Postage Stamp War

The British encampment lay twelve miles south of Ajeebgarh. More than five thousand men were ready to attack, including the Duke of Dumbarton's own Third Foot, from whose ranks the three Tommies had deserted. The soldiers were ready for war—bayonets sharpened, rifles cleaned and oiled, their last letters home written and sealed. An ominous mood of resignation and fear lay over the troops, who knew they would soon be ordered into battle.

Major General Sir Mortimer Somerset-Downs, commander in chief, huddled with his senior officers in a tent lighted by hurricane lanterns. Lt. Col. W. T. Shepherdson, senior aide-de-camp, was explaining that no communication had been received from Hermes, a secret agent sent to Ajeebgarh. He was supposed to have filed a report about the maharajah's trade negotiations with the Russians.

"I can't explain it, sir," said Shepherdson. "Hermes was going to send me a coded message as soon as he got on the *Himalayan*

Mail. When the train came to a level crossing, Hermes was to slip the letter out the window of his compartment. I had two men stationed there to collect it, but the *Himalayan Mail* passed by twelve hours ago and there's no sign of Hermes' dispatch. I can't explain it, sir. He's one of our most reliable agents."

Major General Sir Somerset-Downs, who had lost an ear in the Crimean War, wrinkled his bushy eyebrows and scowled.

"If there's no report from Hermes, then we'll have to attack at dawn," he said. "We shall take Ajeebgarh by force. Prepare your men."

The officers stood up and saluted, leaving the tent in strained silence. Lt. Col. Shepherdson waited until they were gone.

"I'm sorry, sir," he said. "But I still feel there's no reason to attack. Surely this matter of postage stamps can be negotiated. The Russian threat is hardly credible, and Ajeebgarh has no strategic value."

"I need proof, man! Proof!" said the general, scratching his prosthetic ear, which was made of the finest malacca rubber, a pale salmon color that matched the general's complexion. "How do you know your agent hasn't been killed, his message intercepted? Can't trust these Russians, you know. Let them get a toehold in India, next thing you'll find the czar playing croquet in Calcutta. And we'll be drinking our tea out of samovars instead of teapots!"

"Yes, sir!" said Shepherdson, saluting.

As he stepped out of the tent, the ADC stared up at the canopy of stars, as if searching for an answer. The night sky was full of constellations and galaxies but no coded information that Shepherdson could decipher.

He didn't know that Hermes was dead, killed by an anarchist. The letter, which could have prevented the war, was now in the killer's pocket. Disguised as a railway attendant, he had entered the secret agent's compartment, strangled Hermes with a silk handkerchief and pocketed the letter. The assassin was allied with a violent political cult intent on overthrowing all forms of government. Before anyone discovered Hermes' body, the anarchist had jumped down from the *Himalayan Mail* and vanished into the shadows at the next station. In his haste, he discarded his railway uniform but forgot to remove the letter from its pocket.

If only that message had reached Lt. Col. Shepherdson in time, the Postage Stamp War could have been averted. Instead the British attacked Ajeebgarh at dawn with cannons blazing, cavalry charging, and foot soldiers marching with bayonets fixed. Though the maharajah's troops put up a brave defense, they were badly outnumbered and suffered terrible casualties. While Major General Sir Mortimer Somerset-Downs received a medal from the queen, almost everyone else knew that the battle of Ajeebgarh was a brutal mistake—or, as historians put it, a failure of intelligence.

The coat, discarded by the assassin, was later found by a refugee escaping the battle of Ajeebgarh. Unknown to him, the letter was still in the pocket. The refugee then carried Hermes' dispatch all the way to Delhi, where it was stolen by a pickpocket who tossed it on the street. From there the letter passed

149

through a dozen hands and was finally delivered to army headquarters. Unfortunately, by this time Lt. Col. Shepherdson had been killed in the battle of Ajeebgarh. Through an error of judgment on the part of a military postal clerk, the letter was considered personal correspondence and forwarded to his next of kin—a niece from Liverpool, who had recently emigrated to Boston. However, by another twist of fate, her forwarding address was written incorrectly. For this reason, the secret agent's dispatch, which could have prevented a senseless war, lay in the dead-letter bin at the Boston Central Post Office for years. It was eventually retrieved by bony fingers that snapped it up like yellowed chopsticks and deposited it in the unknown postman's mailbag.

30
Trapped

You're going to get us into a lot of trouble," Gil whispered as he crouched down and followed Nargis along the dock. Lights were burning at each corner of the marina and the moon was almost full, but between the lines of moored boats the shadows were as dark as spilled oil.

"Here," said Nargis, stopping a few yards from the end of the dock. A lobster boat was rocking gently on the incoming tide. Before Gil could stop her, Nargis had clambered aboard. He hesitated, crouching next to one of the posts on the dock. It was past nine o'clock and Gil had promised his grandfather he'd be home by ten. He and Nargis had said they were going to a movie at the Cineplex, but instead they were sneaking around the waterfront. Finally, Gil got up the courage to reach out and grab the side of the lobster boat. Throwing one leg over, he climbed inside. Nargis was tugging at something in the back, and all at once there was a crash.

"Are you insane?" said Gil. "What are you doing?"

"Got it," said Nargis, holding up an old lobster trap. Gil could just make out what it was in the dark.

"You're going to steal that?" he said.

"Borrow it," she said.

"For what?"

"Shh!" said Nargis, kneeling down.

A guard with a flashlight was walking down the dock. Gil lowered his head, feeling something wet and slimy under his knees. He didn't want to know what it was. The yellow beam of light moved across the line of boats, illuminating the decks and cabins, probing for the source of the sound. Gil held his breath as the light flickered across the top of the lobster boat, which had a high, square cabin with a brass foghorn. Any second now, he expected the light to flash in his eyes, but after a minute or two the guard turned around. Nargis waited until the door of the marina office closed, then gestured for Gil to follow her. Carrying the lobster trap between them, they made their way quickly to the parking lot where they'd left their bikes. A few days earlier, Gil had fixed up his grandfather's old bicycle, putting air in the tires and oiling the chain. It worked, though there weren't any gears and the bike creaked and groaned.

"Now, will you please tell me why you're stealing a lobster trap?" said Gil as Nargis unlocked her bike.

"I thought you might have figured that out by now," she said. "We're going to catch the spinster's hand."

Balancing the trap on the handlebars in front of her, Nargis set off without waiting for a response. Gil stood there stunned for several moments, then quickly jumped on his bike and began to pedal after her, racing to keep Nargis in sight. Instead of going through the center of Carville, which was brightly lit, she took a back street where they wouldn't be seen. By the time Gil had finally caught up with her, she was already at the cemetery gate.

"This isn't going to work, I'm sure, but what are you planning to do if you actually catch the hand?" said Gil.

Nargis thought for a moment. "We'll show it to your grandfather and prove we weren't lying."

The main gate of the cemetery was locked and there was a large sign: NO ENTRY FROM SUNSET TO SUNRISE. But the wall was only three feet high, and they could easily climb over. After hiding their bikes behind a laurel hedge, Gil and Nargis carried the old lobster trap inside. It wasn't heavy but it was awkward, made of narrow slats of wood, held together with wire and rope mesh. The trap was wet and smelled of fish.

Camellia Stubbs's grave lay under the chestnut tree. When they set the trap down next to her headstone, Gil could just make out her name. Standing in the dark, he felt he was being watched, not from the trees or the street, or even by the moon overhead, but from under the earth, as if there were eyes in the ground staring up at him through the grass.

"Now all we need is some bait," said Nargis, setting the trap. Gil looked at her as she handed him a pen and her homework notebook. "What's this?"

"You said your handwriting is pretty bad. I'm sure she'll try to crumple it up."

"What do I write?" said Gil.

"Anything you like," said Nargis.

It was cold in the graveyard and Gil shivered as a sharp wind blew in off Hornswoggle Bay. His fingers were shaking so badly he didn't have to try to make his handwriting messy, scribbling a few lines on the page. In the dark, he could barely make out his own words:

Roses are red,
Violets are blue,
Everyone's dead,
And so are you.

Tearing out the page, Gil handed it to Nargis, who put the piece of paper inside the trap.

"Okay, let's get out of here," she said. "Tomorrow morning, on my way to school, I'll check and see if we've caught anything."

Gil's hands still smelled from the lobster trap, and the knees of his jeans were wet as they headed toward the gate. He pulled the collar of his parka up to his chin, then started to laugh, first a snicker, then louder, as if he'd just heard a hilarious joke.

"What's wrong with you?" said Nargis, starting to laugh herself, both of them giggling with nervous relief.

Gil tried to catch his breath but the laughter made it impossible for him to speak. Nargis too was in hysterics now and both of them were doubled up, as if they'd just done the stupidest thing in the world, setting a lobster trap for a ghost.

Nargis was laughing so hard, she had tears streaming down her face, and Gil felt as if he was going to collapse. Then, all at once, they stopped.

A clattering noise came from the direction of Camellia's grave. It sounded like somebody rattling a door. Nargis and Gil were still gasping from their laughing fit, but now they were seriously scared. The grin on Gil's face turned into a mask of horror as Nargis grabbed his arm so hard it hurt. The noise grew louder and more insistent, a frenzied knocking and banging followed by a clatter.

"We've caught it!" Nargis said in a choked whisper. Slowly, she let go of Gil's arm.

"N-no way . . . !" he stammered, trembling from the soles of his feet to his scalp.

Though it was the last thing either of them wanted to do, the two turned back and started running in the direction of the sound. When they got to Camellia's grave, there was no sign of the trap. Farther down, near the lower wall of the cemetery, they heard a loud crash and a cracking sound, as if someone were breaking a chair. Without thinking, they hurried down the hill, dodging tombstones and trying to locate the sound. By the time they reached the bottom, everything was silent. In the shadowy moonlight, the two of them looked around, eyes wide with fear, terrified at what they might find.

Feeling as if his legs had turned into rubber bands, Gil saw something lying in the grass. It was part of the trap, two slats of splintered wood and frayed bits of rope. Farther on, Nargis found shredded pieces of paper on which Gil had scribbled his poem. The palms of her hands were sweating even though it was freezing cold. Near the cemetery wall were more scattered remains of the lobster trap. It looked as if it had been torn apart by some kind of wild animal, mangled pieces of wood and wire ripped apart in a furious rage.

31

The Siege of Ajeebgarh

A loud explosion rocks the walls of the house. Sikander lies under his bed, where he has taken shelter, along with his mother and sister. He wonders where his father must be, afraid to think what might have happened to him. As one of the maharajah's bodyguards, Sikander's father must be facing the full brunt of the British assault. Another shell bursts near the house and the ground trembles. Fighting has been going on since dawn and Sikander guesses it must be noon. The air is full of smoke and he can hear the rustle of flames from one of the houses nearby.

Unable to bear it any longer, Sikander squirms out from under the bed. His mother calls to him, but he tells her not to worry. He will find his father, he says, don't be afraid. Pushing aside the table that barricades their front door, Sikander sees the carnage outside, a neighbor's house burned to the ground. Another home has been destroyed by an artillery shell, its roof collapsed and the windows shattered. There is no one on the street. By now the sound of gunfire has subsided to a distant crackling from the northern quarter of the city.

As he makes his way toward the palace, Sikander sees nothing but destruction: a timber merchant's shop on fire, billowing black smoke; a carriage overturned, no sign of the horse; two men carrying a wounded figure to safety; a body slumped across a doorstep.

Ducking as he runs, Sikander moves from the cover of a shattered wall to the flimsy protection of a fallen awning. With a sudden clatter of hooves, two donkeys run past in panic, braying loudly. The sky is dark with smoke, even though it is midday and the smell of burning fires has a sour stench. With a whistling sound, another shell comes in over the rooftops, bursting in the square and leaving a smoldering crater eight feet wide.

Sikander dashes across to the railway station. One of the domes has been destroyed, but the clock is still intact and reads twenty minutes past twelve. Taking a lane into the spice bazaar, Sikander sees bags of red chilies and yellow tumeric spilling into the gutter. Many of the buildings have been ransacked, but the calligrapher's shop remains untouched, its front door sealed with a heavy padlock. Usually the street is crowded with people. Today it is deserted, except for a man who has been wounded. He sits on the ground, staring into space. When Sikander stops to ask if he can help, the man shakes his head as if in a trance and waves the boy away.

But more disturbing than anything he has seen until now are the ruins of the Central Post and Telegraph Office. The whole building has collapsed, smoking like a volcano. Nothing is left of the pillared verandas, the broad steps, or the ornate brickwork along the roof, the high ceilings and the polished brass grilles. All is gone, as if this were the target at which every gun had been aimed. The telegraph wire has snapped off and lies tangled in the rubble.

Sikander has no time to stop. He races toward the river. The bridge has been badly damaged, but enough remains for him to cross over. Another half a mile and he reaches the palace. Here he can see line upon line of armed men in red uniforms—British troops. The firing has stopped and the palace has been captured. Maharajah Lajawab Singh II has surrendered, his flag torn down. The façade of his palace, which once shone pristine white with marble balconies and terraces, is pockmarked with bullet holes and streaked with soot. A group of soldiers are dragging a burning piano out of a door as another group leads a dozen prisoners across the parade ground. Sikander gives a start as he sees his father in the group. Mehboob Khan walks with his head held high. His shirt is bloodstained and his hands are tied behind his back. Sikander begins to shout but stops himself just in time. He knows his father is alive, but there is nothing he can do to help.

Rushing home to tell his mother and his sister, he finds them tending to a neighbor whose house has burned next door. The injured woman lies on a couch as Sikander's mother gives her water to drink and ties a bandage around her bleeding arm. Now that the guns have fallen silent, Sikander can hear wailing throughout the town, voices crying out the names of those who are lost. When he tells his mother that his father has been taken prisoner, she sighs with relief because he is alive, but does not smile.

Feeling helpless and afraid, Sikander slips away to his room. Above their home, pigeons are circling through the smoke. While he was running through the streets, he had been able to hold back his fear. Now that he is home again, he finds his whole body shaking, as if the aftershock of war is worse than the battle itself. From under his pillow he takes the blue bottle. Today, even the bright color of the glass looks dull. With an unsteady hand, he opens an ink pot and picks up a pen. On the back of the note that Gil has sent, Sikander writes a desperate reply, telling his friend that all is lost. Ajeebgarh has been destroyed.

32
More Rhyme Than Reason

You still haven't told me why you got thrown out of school, Grandpa," said Gil.

Prescott looked up from his plate, where the spaghetti had formed a horse's mane against a sunset of tomato sauce.

"What was that?" he asked.

"Why did you get expelled from McCauley?" Gil repeated.

"Oh, that . . . ," said Prescott, taking his fork and turning the noodles into a slippery tornado. "It was a number of things I'd done. The teachers didn't like me very much—'too rebellious, not enough school spirit,' they told my parents. As far as I was concerned McCauley Prep was a pretentious pile of . . ."—he hesitated for a moment before finishing the sentence—". . . horse manure. But the thing that really ticked them off were some of the limericks I wrote about the headmaster and the teachers. That's what finally got me kicked out of school."

"For writing limericks?" said Gil. "That's nothing."

"Well . . . ," said Prescott, taking a bite of food. "These were pretty rude limericks for 1953. Things were a bit more conservative back then. I can't remember all of them, but the headmaster was Archibald Newmann. We called him Starchy Archie, among other things." Pausing a moment, Prescott recited the limerick:

"There once was a headmaster called Newmann,
Whose mind was more floral than human.
While picking his nose,
He dug out a rose,
Crying, 'Egads! My brain is a-bloom'n!' "

Gil laughed. "What does 'Egads' mean?"

"It's an old-fashioned expression that Newmann always used, like 'Oh geez!' " Prescott shook his head. "I can't believe I still remember these limericks. I wrote them more than fifty years ago, when I was your age. We passed them around the school, until one of the teachers found a copy and I was hauled up in front of Newmann. There was a whole series, one about each of the teachers. Here's another that's coming back to me, about our math teacher, who was completely off his rocker:

"There once was a teacher named Bentnick,
Whose behavior was more than eccentric.
When his name was announced,

162

Bentnick pronounced:
'I'm a few sandwiches short of a picnic!' "

"They must have got angry," said Gil, "but writing limericks still doesn't seem serious enough to get you thrown out of school. I mean, it's not something like plagiarism, is it?"

Prescott glanced up at his grandson with a sympathetic expression.

"Maybe not. But I suppose there are worse things than plagiarism too," he said. "What made you do it?"

Gil shook his head, slurping up a forkful of spaghetti before answering.

"I hate writing," he said. "I know what I did was wrong, but I just couldn't write a poem of my own."

"Stealing words isn't quite like stealing money," Prescott said. "But it's still cheating."

"Yeah," said Gil. "I guess I learned my lesson."

"Why do you hate writing?" Prescott asked.

"It's hard. Whatever I write always sounds stupid." Gil shoved his plate aside impatiently. "I mean, for you it must be easy being a writer. But for me, every word I write is painful, like squeezing a zit."

Prescott pointed a finger at Gil and smiled. "If you wrote down what you just said, it would be a great sentence. Squeezing zits is a lot like writing, even for those of us who don't have acne anymore."

"Yeah, but . . ." Gil shook his head in frustration. "It takes so

163

long to write a whole page. Before I even start, it feels as if I'll never get to the end. And then the teachers make us rewrite everything, which is even worse."

"I know what you mean," said Prescott, "but there's a lot of satisfaction in filling a page and knowing those words are yours and nobody else's."

"Maybe," said Gil.

"Poetry is even harder than prose," said Prescott.

"Because you've got to make it rhyme and stuff?" Gil asked.

"Partly that, but you've also got to use fewer words and try to say twice as much in half the space," Prescott explained. He'd finished most of his meal but there was still some food left on his plate. "I mean, look at this spaghetti. How would you describe it in three words or less?"

Gil thought for a moment. "Worms in sauce," he said.

Prescott shook his head. "That's too easy. Not good enough. I want to see it through your eyes and hear it in your words. Try to describe this plate of spaghetti in a way that nobody has ever described it before. Take a minute to think about it."

Gil stared at the smeared red sauce and the long strands of pasta curled together in tangled shapes. He tried to think what it looked like.

"Blood and guts," he said.

Prescott frowned at him. "No. That's a dead metaphor. All you're doing is falling back on words and phrases you've heard before. I want something completely fresh. Surprise me. Make me visualize it through your imagination."

Gil blew out his cheeks in frustration. "It's hard!"

"Of course it is," said Prescott. "But just think how you came up with that simile of squeezing zits. I don't think anybody has ever described the act of writing in exactly those words."

The half-eaten spaghetti stared back at Gil, as if it were a puzzle he had to solve, a riddle without a definite answer.

33
Special Delivery

Shifting gears as she pedaled uphill, Nargis leaned forward, trying to make it to the top without slowing down. As soon as the dirt road descended again, she let herself relax and coasted until she came to a patch of muddy water. Though Nargis could have easily avoided it, there was something satisfying about bicycling straight through a puddle. After another short climb, she skidded around a corner and came to a stop in front of Trash Hill. It was a gray, overcast day, and the mountain of garbage and dead leaves looked like a ruined pyramid. The mailbox stuck out at an angle, its red flag raised.

As Nargis climbed over a pile of broken cinder blocks and the gutted remains of a box spring, she wished that Gil had come with her. She wasn't sure if she really wanted to open the mailbox again. Being alone didn't usually bother her, but today she felt more than a little spooked.

A couple of seagulls circled overhead, their wings catching the air currents off the ocean. *Don't be a chicken*, Nargis said to herself. *It's probably empty.* She sniffed carefully to see if there was any trace of the spinster's hand, but all she could smell was a wet, muddy odor of moldering leaves. As far as she could remember, the red plastic flag had been lowered the last time they were here. Now it stood up like a warning.

Quickly, before she lost her nerve, Nargis reached over and flipped open the front of the mailbox. This time it wasn't empty, but instead of the skeletal hand, she discovered three letters inside. They were stacked neatly side by side, as if someone had carefully arranged them there for Nargis to find. After glancing around to see if anyone might be watching, she took them out and read the addresses. The first was a large, cream-colored envelope. The handwriting was perfect, the graceful lines of each letter flowing together like an ornate design.

From: Camellia Stubbs
4 Hyslop Lane
Hornswoggle Bay

To: Mr. Ezekiel Finch
Upper Finch Tea Estate
Ajeebgarh, India

By the kind hand of:
Captain V. Tobbler

The second envelope was completely different. It was crumpled and badly stained. The handwriting looked childish, as if it were written by an eight-year-old boy who couldn't spell:

URGINT
Frum: Nun o' yer bisniss

To: Mr. Rodrick Sleemin Esq.
Upp'r Finch Tee Estate
AJeebgurh

The third letter was a plain, rectangular envelope, with the address neatly typed.

Confidential
From: Hermes

To: Lt. Col. W. T. Shepherdson

None of the letters had ever been opened, each envelope firmly sealed. There weren't any stamps, though they all seemed to have been carried through time and history. Holding them in her hands, Nargis felt a strange sense of possessing secrets kept for years. Tucking the letters into the front pocket of her sweatshirt, she scrambled back onto her bike and headed straight for the Yankee Mahal.

Gil was outside in the front yard, helping his grandfather trim the yew bushes near the front steps. The first snowfall of

168

the year had long since melted, though the grass was turning brown. Prescott held a pair of pruning shears, while Gil was piling the cuttings into a wheelbarrow. Kipling lay asleep on the front steps. He lifted his head drowsily when Nargis arrived.

"Hey!" said Gil. "What's up?"

"Nothing much," said Nargis, though he could see from the expression on her face that she was dying to tell him something.

Prescott nodded to his grandson. "I'll finish up here. You can go inside."

The two of them went around to the kitchen door and straight upstairs to the study with the rolltop desk. Nargis put the three letters down triumphantly.

"What's this?" asked Gil.

"These were in the mailbox on Trash Hill," she said.

"You're kidding." Gil cautiously picked them up.

"No, I'm not." Nargis grinned. "I just came from there. We should open them."

"I don't know," said Gil. "We don't want to find any more genies, do we?"

"Yeah, but these are obviously meant for us. They must be letters that never reached the people they were written for. I'm sure the spinster's hand left them." Nargis reached for the letter opener that lay in one of the pigeonholes inside the desk. The miniature scimitar shone in her hand.

"Which one first?" asked Gil.

"This one. It's from Camellia Stubbs. Check out her handwriting . . ."

"Yeah, but if we open it, maybe her hand will come after us."

"I don't think so," Nargis said, taking the envelope and slicing it open before Gil could stop her. When she took out the letter, it was covered in the same handwriting, but before they could read what was written, a lock of brown hair fell onto the desk. It was tied with a pale pink ribbon.

"What is it?" Gil asked.

"What does it look like?" she said. "Somebody's hair."

Gil made a face. "That's gross."

"Not as gross as a skeleton's hand."

After reading the love letter, they picked the letter from Hermes next, with the typed address. Again the scimitar cut smoothly through the paper, with a dry whispering sound.

"Sick! More hair!" said Gil.

"Looks like a caterpillar." Nargis poked at it with the paper knife.

"No, it's a fake moustache."

"Now, that's disgusting."

"But look at the message. It doesn't make any sense."

"Must be some kind of code."

Unable to decipher the message, they picked up the third envelope. "This one looks like something Kipling might have found," said Gil, sniffing it.

"Some kid must have written it," Nargis added. "I'm surprised the spinster's hand hasn't crumpled it up."

This time the blade of the letter opener didn't slip in as smoothly, and tore a ragged line along the fold. There was hair inside this envelope too, a handful of red curls that looked as if they'd never been combed. Brushing these onto the desk beside the neatly tied brown lock and the black moustache, Nargis squinted at the awkward writing.

"The ransom note!" she said.

34

Rest in Peace

For the past two days, Kipling had been listless. When Gil tried to get him to go for a walk, he wagged his tail but refused to go beyond the yard. He didn't seem interested in eating, either, which was unusual. Sunday morning he was sprawled on the kitchen floor, in his favorite place next to the radiator. When Gil headed out the door to rake leaves in the backyard, he noticed the old dog's feet were twitching and he gave a couple of muffled barks, probably dreaming that he was chasing a postman.

Within an hour, Kipling died in his sleep. Prescott found him when he came into the kitchen to make a cup of coffee. He noticed Kip wasn't breathing. Kneeling down and placing a hand on his side, Prescott knew it was over. After a few minutes alone, he went outside and called Gil, who could tell something was wrong from the tone of his grandfather's voice.

"Kip sounded wheezy this morning," said Prescott, blowing his nose into a checkered handkerchief. "I was thinking about taking him to the vet."

Gil stared down at the lifeless dog. He felt awful and wanted to say something to comfort his grandfather but couldn't speak for a minute or two.

"How old was he?" Gil asked at last.

"Fourteen," said Prescott. "Almost a hundred in human years."

"He was barking in his sleep when I came past him this morning," said Gil.

"Must have had a heart attack." Prescott put a hand on his grandson's shoulder. "If you've got to go, there isn't a better way . . ."

"What are we going to do?" Gil said.

"I guess we should bury him. Sooner the better," Prescott said. "I'll get something to wrap Kip in, and you can bring the shovel from the garden shed. We'll find a place out back."

Gil was glad to get outdoors. He felt a little dizzy, and the clean fall air was cold in his lungs. He choked back his tears as he walked across the leaf-littered lawn, half of which he'd raked into piles. Though he'd known the dog for only a couple of weeks, it seemed as if he'd lost a friend. Gil felt much worse for his grandfather, knowing how close he'd been to Kipling. Even if the dog went peacefully in his sleep, it seemed a terrible thing to happen, so suddenly without any warning. Gil couldn't stop thinking of Kip's paws kicking less than an hour ago, as if he were trying to run in his sleep. Now he was gone.

When Prescott came out, his eyes were red and swollen. Just looking at his grandfather, Gil felt a lump in his throat.

Awkwardly, they walked around the edge of the yard, trying to find a place to bury Kipling.

"Maybe back there," said Prescott, pointing to a stand of birches with papery white trunks. A couple of gold leaves still clung to the thin branches, but otherwise the trees were bare.

Gil raked away the dead foliage. After choosing a spot where there weren't too many rocks, he began to dig. At first it was easy, the shovel plunging into the soft layers of mulch and earth, but after he got down a foot or more, there were rocks and tree roots. He and his grandfather took turns. It was a relief having something to do, the exertion of digging clearing his mind. Gil had never dug a grave before, and it felt strange, knowing that this was where Kipling would soon be laid to rest. It wasn't a very large hole, two feet across and three feet long, but the deeper it got, the harder it was to shovel out the dirt.

"Another six inches," said Prescott as Gil wiped the sweat off his face. "Do you want me to take over?"

"No, I'm fine," said Gil, feeling the shovel strike something hard. "Here's another stone."

He dug around it first, so he could slide the blade underneath, then pried it up. But as soon as he saw what he'd unearthed, Gil stopped abruptly.

"Geez!" he said softly.

Prescott let out a low whistle.

As he lifted the shovel, more of the dirt fell away, revealing a rectangular box. Without saying anything, Prescott reached out and took it, then brushed away the rest of the soil. When he opened the box, Gil blinked in astonishment and caught his breath. Inside was the gold inkstand from the portrait of Ezekiel Finch. Even though it had lain underground for more than a century, the rubies and emeralds glinted in the autumn sunlight.

Gil and his grandfather stared at each other with amazement, stunned by what they'd found. Prescott finally closed the box and set it on the ground.

"First things first," he said softly, turning toward the house. Gil shoveled out a few more inches of earth and glanced back to see his grandfather come out of the Yankee Mahal, carrying Kipling's body wrapped in a gray blanket. Neither of them spoke as the dog was laid in the ground.

"So long, old friend," said Prescott.

"Bye, Kip," said Gil.

Each of them tossed a handful of earth into the grave, then Prescott picked up the shovel and began to fill in the hole. After a few minutes, Gil took over again and shoveled the pile of earth on top of the dog, burying him forever in the ground.

35
Terms of Surrender

Today, the ink that Sikander makes, according to the calligrapher's instructions, is blended from the black residue scraped out of the mouth of a cannon. It has an acrid, sulfurous stench as Sikander grinds the burnt powder with his mortar and pestle. He also adds the charred remains of a scrap of blackened timber that he picked from the ruins of Ajeebgarh's post office. This is mixed with the juice of a bitter gourd and clear resin from a coffin-wood tree. The color of the ink reflects the dark pall lying over Ajeebgarh today, a black mood of fear and defeat. Against his wishes, Ghulam Rusool, the calligrapher, has been ordered to write the terms of the maharajah's surrender, as dictated by Major General Sir Mortimer Somerset-Downs. It must be written both in English and Urdu, so that all who can read will understand that Lajawab Singh II has relinquished his throne.

Among the various terms and conditions under which the maharajah surrenders, he will never again be permitted the prestige of issuing his own postage stamps. Henceforward, all mail sent or delivered to Ajeebgarh will carry postage that bears Queen Victoria's profile instead of the maharajah's turbaned visage. In addition to this, whatever tea is produced in Ajeebgarh can be sold only to British traders, and all economic and political connections with Russia are severed.

Though Lajawab Singh's life will be spared, he is exiled to an island off the coast of Nova Scotia, far away from his native state. But of all the terms of surrender that make the hands of the calligrapher's apprentice shake, as he stirs the ingredients for this fatal ink, the worst is that the maharajah's bodyguards will be executed. His father and the other men who remained loyal to their king will be tied across the mouths of cannons, day after tomorrow, and shot at dawn. Sikander feels all is lost. Staring into the stone mortar full of ink, he cannot find even a glimmer of hope. When he finally pours the black liquid into the calligrapher's ink pot and arranges the pens and paper for this tragic document, Sikander sets aside a little of the ink for himself. Retreating to the back of the shop, he takes a slip of paper and writes a desperate note to Gil.

Then he picks up the blue bottle from under a pile of rags, where he hid it yesterday after retrieving the last message. Walking alone through the smoldering ruins of Ajeebgarh, he takes a shortcut past a graveyard, which seems more alive than the city itself. Those who died in the siege of Ajeebgarh are buried here beneath freshly turned mounds of earth. Other casualties have been cremated on the banks of the Magor River. As Sikander reaches the temples and shrines that overlook the burning ghats, funeral pyres are burning. Those who were injured during the attack have succumbed to their wounds. Everything he sees today reminds him of death.

When Sikander finally arrives on the riverbank, he already has tears in his eyes. The slow-moving current is blurred and the glass bottle in his hand seems to melt within his vision. Sikander thinks of his lost friend Lawrence and the British cannons that await his father. In a gesture of anger and anguish, he jams the cork into the throat of the bottle and hurls it out into the river.

36
The Inkstand

Lenore drove across to the Yankee Mahal as soon as Prescott called to tell her about Kipling's death. She brought some roses, which she placed on the dog's grave. When they came back into the kitchen, Prescott put water on for tea and made them each a cup. A few minutes later, he brought out the inkstand to show Lenore and explained where it had been found.

"Do you think those are real rubies and emeralds?" Gil asked. He was almost afraid to touch it.

"Must be," said Lenore. "And these blue stones are sapphires."

"The stand is solid gold," said Prescott. "Feel the weight."

"What are you going to do with it?" Gil asked.

Prescott shook his head. "I have no idea."

Taking one of the crystal ink pots, which looked like a huge diamond, Lenore held it up to the light. The ink pot was like a prism, its polished facets refracting a rainbow of colors.

"It must be worth a ton of money," said Gil.

"Priceless," said Lenore.

"It belongs in a museum," Prescott added.

Even though they were all amazed by the beauty and extravagance of the inkstand, they were still subdued by what had happened to Kip. Seeing his feeding bowl on the kitchen floor, Gil felt a sudden ache of sadness. In a weird way, it seemed as if, even in death, Kipling had led them to the inkstand, just as he led them to the old mailbox and the spinster's hand. Lenore turned the stand around and read aloud an inscription on the back:

For my Darling Camellia
Whose words are as precious as jewels
and as pure as gold.

"Ezekiel must have loved her very much," said Lenore.

"It's a shame she never got to see this inkstand," said Prescott. "He was going to give it to her as an engagement gift, but then she turned him down."

Gil almost said something about the lost letters that Nargis had found, especially the one from Camellia, but he didn't know how Prescott and Lenore would react, and he wasn't sure how to explain it all.

This time, after they drank their tea, Lenore didn't read the leaves. Instead, she let Gil put the cups in the dishwasher. Just as he was finishing, the doorbell rang. Gil knew it must be Nargis. After letting her in, he explained what had happened.

"That's awful! Poor Kip . . . ," said Nargis. "I can't believe it. Should I come back later?"

"No, it's all right," said Gil.

Nargis followed him to the kitchen.

"I'm really sorry about your dog...," she started to say. Prescott gave her a sad smile as Lenore reached out and hugged her. Just then, Nargis noticed the gold inkstand on the kitchen counter.

"Whoa!" she said under her breath. "Where did that come from?"

Gil caught her eye. "We found this in the backyard when we were burying Kip."

Nargis touched the gold inkstand, running her fingers over the intricate workmanship and the precious jewels. When Lenore explained that it was supposed to have been a gift for Camellia, Nargis turned to Gil.

"Have you shown them the letters?" she asked.

"Not yet," he said, hesitating. "Should I?"

"I think so." Nargis nodded.

Prescott and Lenore looked puzzled as Gil headed upstairs to the rolltop desk, where they had left the letters in a pigeon-hole. Meanwhile, Nargis told them how she had found the three sealed envelopes in the old mailbox on Trash Hill.

When Gil returned, Prescott and Lenore unfolded Camellia's letter first and read it together silently. Gil and Nargis exchanged an uncertain glance. When he finished, Prescott asked to see the envelope.

"Are you sure this is real?" he asked.

"I don't know," said Nargis. "Who else would have written it?"

"There are two more letters," Gil added. "One is a ransom note and the other is written in some kind of code."

As Prescott and Lenore studied the Tommy's scribbled, misspelled note and the strange typewritten words, Nargis nudged Gil.

"Tell them about the bottle," she urged.

Taking a deep breath, he explained how he'd been sending messages back and forth to Sikander. Gil could see the look of suspicion in his grandfather's eyes, but Prescott didn't speak until Gil finished.

"What bottle is this?" he asked.

"The blue gripe-water bottle I showed you last week—remember? I didn't say anything about the messages because I didn't think you'd believe me," Gil confessed.

"Where's the bottle now?" asked Prescott.

"I threw it into the ocean yesterday but I haven't got a reply. I can show you Sikander's messages if you like," said Gil.

Prescott tugged at his moustache uncertainly as Gil ran back up to his room. Lenore was trying to decipher the coded words that Hermes had written. She thought they might be anagrams and was trying to juggle the letters. A few minutes later, Gil spread all of Sikander's handwritten messages on the kitchen counter beside the inkstand. Prescott inspected them carefully.

"So, you're trying to tell me these were written more than a hundred years ago?" he said with a skeptical frown. "Is there any way to prove it?"

"Come on, Prescott, why would they be making all this up?" said Lenore. She seemed almost convinced.

Gil stared at both of them helplessly. "Sikander wrote to us about his friend Lawrence being kidnapped. He sent us this newspaper clipping. And look, the letter Nargis found must be the ransom note . . ."

"If only there was some way we could send these letters back in history," Nargis interrupted. "Maybe Ezekiel Finch would change his mind, and Lawrence could be freed."

"But that's impossible," said Prescott.

"I don't know," said Gil. "Sikander has been writing to us about the battle of Ajeebgarh. The British army has invaded the city . . . I mean, they attacked a hundred years ago. But for Sikander it's happening right now."

Prescott began to shake his head.

"You have to believe us, Mr. Finch," said Nargis. "We aren't lying. There's also a genie . . ."

Hearing this, even Lenore looked doubtful.

"Genie?" said Prescott, without any attempt to hide his disbelief.

"We tried to show you the other day," Gil blurted out. "But he wouldn't rise off the page. His name is Aristo and you have to read this poem aloud to call him."

Prescott picked up Camellia's letter again and frowned. "This certainly looks genuine enough and could be a letter Camellia Stubbs wrote, but all this stuff about messages in a bottle traveling back and forth through time . . . And now you want me to believe in a genie?"

"We'd call him up for you," said Gil, his voice growing desperate. "But it's Sunday and he takes the weekends off."

Lenore and Prescott exchanged doubtful looks.

"It's true," Nargis said in frustration. "It's really, honestly true!"

"All right," said Prescott, putting up both hands. "I'm not saying either of you is lying, but maybe your imaginations have got the best of you. The only thing we have here are a lot of random letters and messages. Maybe they fit together. Maybe not . . ."

As his voice trailed off, Lenore spoke up. "Wait a minute; I know this sounds crazy, but I believe them."

"Of course you would," said Prescott, rolling his eyes.

"No, but don't you see?" said Lenore. "It all makes sense. Gil's star sign is governed by Mercury, the messenger. That's why these letters have come to him. If he can deliver them, like Nargis said, then maybe he can help his friend Sikander and bring Ezekiel and Camellia together again!"

Gil frowned, not completely sure what she meant.

"It's exactly what I predicted," said Lenore. "It was written in the tea leaves, and on the palm of his hand, just as it's there in his horoscope. Gil is the messenger. To be a peacemaker, to save a life, to offer the key of love, he has to send these letters back in time."

"Okay," said Nargis. "But how?"

37

Scrambled Alphabet

That night Gil had trouble falling asleep. He tried to read a novel his grandfather had given him, but his eyes kept wandering off the page and anxiously tracing the patterns in the wallpaper next to his bed, as if it were a puzzle he needed to solve. When he finally turned off the light, he tossed and turned for almost an hour and finally dozed off into unsettled dreams. He found himself in a place he'd never been before—it could have been India—though parts of it were familiar, like the buildings of his old school. He was sitting in a classroom and listening to a teacher who looked like Aristo, except the teacher had legs. Suddenly, there in front of him on the desk was the blue bottle. As quietly as possible, he tried to uncork the bottle, but it made a loud popping noise, like champagne. Everyone in the classroom turned to look at him. Something was spilling out of the bottle, and he tried to keep it from overflowing by holding his thumb over the mouth. Then all at once, he wasn't in the classroom anymore, and instead of the bottle he was holding a scimitar in his hand . . .

That was when he woke up, tossing the covers aside in a panic and sitting up in bed with alarm. Glancing across at the clock on his bedside table, he saw it was five minutes past midnight. Gil fell back onto his pillow and stared up into the darkness, glad to escape the dream. At that moment, he heard a tapping sound. It was a bit like water dripping, but louder and not as steady. *Tik . . . Tdikh . . . Tik . . .*

Except for this sound, the Yankee Mahal was completely silent. Gil listened as he lay there, wondering if it was the radiators clicking. *Tdikh. Tdikh. Tik Tik. Tdikh. Tik.* It wasn't a clock, though it sounded a bit like that. Or it could have been a bird pecking at one of the gutters along the roof. Very slowly, Gil got out of bed and opened the door into the hallway. The sound was louder now. *Tdikh. Tika tik . . . Tdikh.* It was coming from downstairs. He listened a minute longer, feeling his bare feet getting cold on the stone floor. *Tdikh . . . Tdikh.* He suddenly recognized the sound. A typewriter! *Tik tik tikka tik.* Prescott must be awake, working on a poem.

Slowly, Gil stepped out into the hall and made his way to the landing. The house was in darkness, though he could see a dim glow from his grandfather's office downstairs. The sound of typing continued, pausing for a few seconds, then resuming, as if the words were emerging slowly from the poet's mind.

The stone steps didn't creak but Gil held the banister as he went down. He could see a crack of light under Prescott's office door, which was slightly ajar. No other lights were on in the house. Gil almost expected Kipling to come padding up behind him, but then he remembered . . .

Without knocking, he pushed open the door, then stopped abruptly. The desk lamp was on, but his grandfather's chair was empty. Gil heard the clicking of the typewriter keys, but nobody seemed to be in the room. Then he smelled a familiar odor and, at the same moment, saw something that made him clench his teeth. The skeletal hand was poised above the typewriter keys and one of its bony fingers tapped a couple of letters. *Tdhik . . . Tdhik . . .*

All at once the hand must have sensed Gil's presence. It jumped like a grotesque grasshopper, off the desk and through the open window. From where he stood, rigid with fear, Gil could just make out the spectral shape of the hand disappearing across the moonlit lawn. A lingering stench of perfumed decay filled the room.

When he finally got up the courage to go near the typewriter, Gil found a poem typed on the page:

Once upon a midnight dreary, while I pondered, weak
    and weary,
Over many a quaint and curious volume of forgotten
    lore—
While I nodded, nearly napping, suddenly there came a
    tapping,
As of some one gently rapping, rapping at my chamber
    door.

"'T is some visiter," I muttered, "tapping at my chamber door—
Only this and nothing more."

Immediately, he recognized the first stanza of "The Raven"
by Edgar Allan Poe, which his teacher had assigned in English
class last fall. Typed beneath the stanza was a separate line:

Ponder no more! These Keys unlock a scrambled
   Alphabet . . .

He shuddered at the memory of the ticking sounds. The
spinster's hand was trying to leave him a message, Gil felt sure
of that, but there didn't seem to be any meaning in the words.

The circular keys on Prescott's typewriter were in the same
order as on a computer keyboard, though several of the letters
had been worn off from years of use. The dented surfaces fit
Gil's fingertips, and when he gently pressed them, he could feel
the springs and levers poised to write. Remembering the bony
fingers picking out the letters, Gil abruptly pulled back both
hands and glanced up at the portrait of Camellia Stubbs on
the wall. In the picture, she was touching the black lace collar
of her blouse with four long, pale fingers and a thumb. Gil
tried to imagine how this woman had lived her whole life alone
after Ezekiel sailed away. It seemed so pointless that she had
wasted all those years, just because of a lost letter.

Gil couldn't understand why anyone would ruin their life like
that, but as he looked at Camellia's face, he could see the tragic

determination in her eyes. Lowering his own eyes to the typed lines on the page, Gil tried to figure out again what the words meant. He wondered if he should show it to Prescott, though he knew his grandfather would think it was another practical joke, like the mailbox, the gripe-water bottle and the genie. He certainly wasn't going to believe that the spinster's hand had typed these words in the middle of the night.

Pulling the paper out of the typewriter, Gil folded it in half and headed back up to his room. The stone floors and steps felt colder underfoot, and he kept looking behind him in the shadows until he was safely back in bed. Lying under the covers with the light still on, Gil read the stanza of poetry over and over again, followed by the cryptic line. "Ponder no more! These Keys unlock a scrambled Alphabet . . ." Maybe, if he hadn't interrupted the hand, it would have left a more complete message. Eventually, the repetition made Gil fall asleep, but even in his dreams the riddle circled through his mind, as he saw himself sitting at the typewriter, fingers flying over the keys as he typed and typed, unable to stop. After a while, when he looked down at the keys, Gil realized it wasn't a typewriter but a skeleton on which his fingers were drumming, the keys like knuckles and the levers like ivory bones radiating out of a severed wrist.

38
Reveille

A military academy! Mom, you've got to be kidding!"

"Your father and I have decided, this is the best school for you . . ."

"No, it isn't. I don't want to learn how to march and salute and shoot a gun. I just want to go back to seventh grade like everybody else. The last thing I'm planning to do is join the army." Gil let out his breath in exasperation.

"Howitzer Academy is a very prestigious school. A lot of their students get accepted at the best universities. It doesn't mean you have to join the army, but it might teach you some discipline."

"Yeah, like boot camp. You know I quit Cub Scouts after three days."

Still holding the phone to his ear, Gil gently pounded his forehead against the wall.

"Gilbert! We had a lot of trouble getting you admitted to

Howitzer. I had to go and personally meet the commandant. They don't usually take students midway through a semester, but he's made an exception."

This time Gil knocked his head a little harder.

"Commandant! It sounds like I'm going to be a prisoner of war. I can't believe this! It's worse than McCauley. How could you do this to me? Where is this place?"

"It's in Michigan," his mother said, her voice strained. "On the Upper Peninsula, a beautiful campus surrounded by woods, on the shores of Lake Superior."

"Michigan? The Upper Peninsula?" Gil groaned. "That's worse than Alaska. It's winter eight months of the year."

"This is for your own good, Gil. Remember, you brought it upon yourself."

Now he threw himself back on his bed.

"Yeah, right. I'm guilty as charged, but that doesn't mean I have to face a court-martial. Forget it, Mom! I'll have to wear a uniform!"

"I think you'll look very nice. When I was there the cadets were all lined up on the parade ground, and it made me so proud just thinking you'd be one of them."

"No way! There's no way I'm going to a school like that. I'd rather just drop out and work at Happy Sundae for the rest of my life."

"Gilbert! Now listen to me. It's all been decided. Your father and I are coming up on Friday and we'll drive you home, then fly to Michigan on Saturday. Make sure you've got everything packed. No arguments. No complaints. This is the best thing that could happen to you."

✦   ✦   ✦

After Gil hung up, it took him several minutes before he could think straight. In his worst nightmares, he hadn't imagined that this was going to happen. *How could his parents do this to him?* Howitzer Academy. It sounded like the sort of place where they lined you up and shot you at dawn. *Yes, sir! No, sir! Ready, aim, fire, sir!*

As soon as he calmed down enough to call Nargis, Gil began to try to figure out how he was going to get out of this mess. Fortunately, Nargis was at home, and by the time he reached her house, she already had the Web site for Howitzer Academy pulled up on her computer screen. Nargis saluted and grinned at him as he came into her room.

"It's not funny!" he said.

"I think you'll look great with red stripes down your pants. And I can't wait to see the haircut . . ."

"Shut up!" he said. "You may think it's a big joke, but somehow I've got to figure some way out of this."

Nargis's expression turned serious.

"Why don't you just go to school here in Carville?" she said. "You can keep on living with your grandfather."

"Yeah, I know, but my parents don't want me going to a public school. They think it's beneath them."

"But Carville has a good school. You'll like my teacher, Mrs. Ballantine. Why don't we go and speak to the principal tomorrow? I'm sure it will be fine and your grandfather will probably agree."

"Yeah. But once my parents get an idea in their heads, they never back down. They're coming to get me on Friday."

Nargis glanced over at the computer screen, which had pictures of Howitzer Academy. The main building looked like a prison with high walls and barred windows. There were two cannons out front. Instead of dorms they had barracks. Scrolling down the site, Nargis clicked on the daily schedule, which began with reveille at six each morning, a three-mile run, shoe polishing for half an hour and classes from eight to four, with only fifteen minutes for lunch. After school there were obstacle courses and drills at the firing range. Dinner was at five thirty sharp, followed by two hours of homework and lights out at eight.

"You have to go to bed at eight o'clock!" said Nargis.

"Yeah, and you have to wake up at six!" Gil added.

"And no girls allowed!" Nargis winked at him.

For a moment, Gil didn't answer. Then he put his head in his hand. "This sounds worse and worse."

"Wait," said Nargis. "Before you start feeling too sorry for yourself, what are we going to do about the letters?"

"I don't know," said Gil in despair. "I don't care what Lenore says, I'm not some sort of messenger!"

Tapping the keys on her computer, Nargis entered the search word *Ajeebgarh*. For the past few days she'd been surfing the Internet, trying to find some explanation or answer to what was going on. Ajeebgarh brought up all kinds of articles and references, from a PhD dissertation by a history professor at the University of Wisconsin to a Web site called Ajeebgarh .com, which had a couple of old photographs of the town in 1898, with British troops occupying the palace. There was even a reference to Ajeebgarh in a rap song by a British boy band, that didn't seem to have anything to do with anything at all. Though the computer gave them random bits of information, none of it seemed as if it would help solve their problem.

The blue bottle stood empty next to the computer, its scuffed glass catching the light from the screen. Sikander's last message lay unfolded beside it, along with the letters.

"What are you going to write back?" asked Nargis.

"What can I say?" Gil said. "I mean, 'Sorry to hear about your war' sounds kind of pathetic."

Placing his fingers on the keyboard of the computer, Gil remembered the typewriter keys, the round steel rims and dented surfaces. He looked down at the letters and typed in "A. K. Jaddoowalla's Gripe Water," then clicked on *search*. The computer took a few seconds to digest the phrase but all that came up on the screen was the message

UNABLE TO LOCATE THIS TERM. TRY ANOTHER KEYWORD.

It was almost as if the genie were inside the computer, frustrating all of their attempts to solve the problem.

"I still can't figure out what this letter means," said Gil, picking up the envelope containing the false moustache.

"It's obviously some kind of code," said Nargis. "Maybe if you type it into the computer . . ."

Gil stared at the garbled letters for a moment—ZGH LTEKTZ—then glanced down at the keyboard on the computer.

"Hey! Wait a minute," he said. "I've got an idea. Look at what was typed by the spinster's hand. 'Ponder no more! These Keys unlock a scrambled Alphabet.'"

Nargis peered over his shoulder, not sure what he meant. "I don't get it," she said.

"This message is written in a scrambled alphabet," said Gil. "The key is the typewriter keyboard."

"Okay . . . ," said Nargis, still uncertain.

"If you replace the letters on the keys with the letters of the alphabet in the correct order, it gives us the code. Instead of *Q* it's *A*. And *W* is *B*. Take the first word of the message: *Z* is *T*, *G* is *O* and *H* is *P*." With each letter, he pointed at the keys. "That spells *TOP*."

They did the same with the second word.

"Secret," said Nargis. "TOP SECRET."

After that, they wrote down the letters on the keyboard and underneath they wrote the alphabet:

QWERTYUIOP
ASDFGHJKL
ZXCVBNM

ABCDEFGHIJ
KLMNOPQRS
TUVWXYZ

Using the keys they quickly unscrambled the message.

TOP SECRET
I HAVE MET WITH VILLANOV. HE ASSURES ME
RUSSIA HAS NO INTEREST IN AJEEBGARH TEA.
NO NEED TO DECLARE WAR.
REGARDS, HERMES

When they were finished, Nargis read the words aloud.

"I bet this message never got sent," said Gil. "That's why there was a war. If it had reached whoever was supposed to get it, they would never have attacked Ajeebgarh."

39
Shattered Hopes

"Grandpa, how can I become a conscientious objector?"

Prescott looked up from the stamps he was studying under a magnifying glass and blinked at Gil, baffled by his grandson's question.

"Why would you want to do that?" he asked.

"My parents are going to put me in a military school—Howitzer Academy," Gil explained.

His grandfather frowned. "When did you hear this?"

"Mom called this afternoon," said Gil. "They're coming to get me on Friday. Grandpa, I really don't want to go! Maybe I could just stay here with you . . . if you'll let me . . . and I can go to school in Carville."

"Well, let's see . . . ," his grandfather started to say, but before he could finish, Gil interrupted.

"I promise I won't make up any more stories about skeletal hands and genies," he said.

"So, you're saying that was all made up?" Prescott asked with a serious expression.

Gil hesitated. "No. I guess I didn't make it up, but I'll never mention it again."

"Truth is, I really don't mind if you're seeing things or even imagining them," Prescott said. "But as for staying here, we'll have to talk to your parents about that."

"I thought if I told them I'm a pacifist like you, then they might not force me to go to Howitzer."

His grandfather grinned. "I'm not sure you'll have to take it that far," he said. "Remember, conscientious objectors sometimes get sent to jail, which is a whole lot worse than a military academy."

Gil kept quiet for a moment. "You don't believe in war?" he asked.

Prescott shook his head. "It never seems to solve anything, as far as I can see."

Gil thought of the message he'd received from Sikander about the destruction of Ajeebgarh.

"Even if I wasn't just trying to get out of going to military school," he said, "I think I'd become a conscientious objector."

"I hope you never have to make that choice," said Prescott. "Now, let's think of other ways to persuade your parents to let you stay here."

"Do you think I really can?" said Gil.

"I'll speak to your mother," Prescott assured him. "Of

course, she's never listened to me before, but I'll give it a try and do everything I can."

✦   ✦   ✦

Later that day, when Gil went down to Rattle Beach, the blue bottle lay in a tidal pool, along with a couple of sea urchins and a yellow starfish. He stared at the bottle for a while before picking it up, thinking how it must have been washed onto the rocks by the waves and how it had been carried through history, over a hundred years. Gil planned to take the bottle home with him and show it to his grandfather, hoping that Prescott would believe him at last. But first he wanted to read the message it contained. Sometimes he wished he could meet Sikander face-to-face, instead of just writing back and forth to him. But that seemed even more impossible than exchanging messages in a gripe-water bottle.

Though the tide was out, the sea was rough, and it looked as if it might snow again. The clouds were rumpled against the horizon like the surf. Staring out at the waves, Gil wondered what it would be like to sail across the Atlantic and travel all the way to India. Of course, now he could fly there in a jet, not like Ezekiel Finch, whose clipper ships took months to circle all the way around Africa. Gil had never thought of taking a journey like that before, but now it seemed like something he might enjoy—discovering new countries and places, hearing different languages spoken . . .

and escaping from military school. Until recently, he'd been happy just to stay near home, but staring out at the waves, he felt an urge to go somewhere far away, somewhere he'd never been before.

When he finally picked the bottle up, Gil had to brush off strands of kelp that were wrapped around its neck. The glass was slippery and cold, like a seashell. The cork felt tighter than before. At first he couldn't get it open, then Gil held the bottle up to look inside. There was a scroll of paper, another message from Sikander.

Gil took the cork between his fingers again and tried to twist it off. All at once, the bottle slid from his grasp. He felt it falling and desperately tried to catch it. But before he could do anything, the bottle of A. K. Jaddoowalla's Finest Indian Gripe Water fell on the rocks and shattered into a dozen pieces. Gil's breath stuck in his throat. He wanted to shout, but no words came out. For several long seconds, he looked down in horror at the jagged blue shards upon the rocks.

Finally, with a sense of despair, he picked up the scroll of paper and read Sikander's words.

Dear Gil,

I need your help! The war is over but we have worse news. My father and the other body-guards are going to be executed day after tomorrow at dawn. Please do anything you *can . . . anything! Please try! I'm waiting for your answer.*

Your friend,
Sikander

The slip of paper rustled in the ocean breeze as Gil stared down at the broken bottle at his feet. He felt as if time itself had shattered—the end of the world.

40
Rewriting History

Tucked inside his envelope, Aristophanes Smith lay upon the page, contemplating metaphysical questions. At this particular moment, he was nothing more than three stanzas of poetry penned with calligrapher's ink. Those magical ingredients that Sikander had mixed together a century ago—charred seeds of a custard apple, ashes from a water pipe smoked by a wandering dervish, soot from a genie's lamp, and a measure of gooseberry wine—provided the only physical substance out of which he was composed. In quiet moments of self-absorbed reflection, which sometimes lasted for years, the genie often wondered who he actually was. Though the ink, from which he was made, gave him shape and form, it was the poetry that brought him to life. *Am I a product of crude* chemistry? he asked himself with a philosophical grimace. *Nothing more than carbon residues emulsified with an adhesive that fixes itself upon the blank surface of a sheet of paper?* The genie shuddered at the thought. *Or . . . am I a product of pure language?'* he mused with a smile.

The lyrical spirit within a poet's words? A fundamental conundrum . . .
Who am I and why am I here?

His thoughts were rudely interrupted as the paper was quickly taken out of the envelope and flattened on a desk by two impatient hands. Blinded by a bright electric light, the genie felt exposed and vulnerable. He heard a girl's voice rapidly reading the poem aloud. "Awake! for morning in the bowl of Night . . ."

Gradually, he felt himself disintegrating, the particles of India ink evaporating as the voice continued. It was a bit like feeling the circulation returning to his limbs, a tingling sensation, as if the poetry were distilled through his veins.

"Nor all thy Tears wash out a Word of it . . ."

Here was the part he never enjoyed. The girl's voice read the final line.

Poof!

Every time he materialized, the genie felt as if he were being scraped off the page. Aristo sneezed as he took on his genie's form, then straightened his lapels and made sure his cravat was correctly positioned between the starched collars of his shirt.

"Yes, m'lady. Your wish is my command!" he said with a polite cough.

Nargis, who was holding the blank sheet of paper, set it aside and stared at him suspiciously. Gil, who didn't look particularly happy today, seemed equally concerned. At the same time, Aristo became aware of two other people in the room. An older gentleman was leaning against the door frame of the study with a shocked expression on his face. The other person was a white-haired woman who looked equally surprised. Aristo bowed toward the two adults politely.

"We need your help right away!" said Nargis.

"Of course," the genie replied. "But allow me first to introduce myself. Aristophanes Smith. Do I have the honor of addressing Mr. Prescott Finch?"

"Yes," said Prescott, swallowing hard, "and this is Lenore Sullivan."

"An honor," said Aristo. "It isn't every day one meets a distinguished poet. If you allow me, I shall recite Tennyson's 'Charge of the Light Brigade,' one of the great monuments of nineteenth-century verse."

"Forget it! We don't have time for that," said Nargis.

Lenore glanced over at Prescott, her eyebrows raised.

"We need you to deliver some messages," said Gil. "These are letters that need to go back to India, over a hundred years ago."

"Oh, I couldn't possibly do that!" said the genie. "We have a very strict policy about tampering with history. No interference with the past. It's a cardinal rule. Absolutely forbidden!"

"Says who?" demanded Nargis. "If we can make something better, I don't see what's wrong with that. Who makes up these rules anyway?"

"It's just the way we operate, our code of conduct, established by the Fraternal Brotherhood of Djinns," said Aristo, folding his arms and fiddling with one of his cuff links. "We don't intrude on historical events. If you change one thing, then everything else begins to change. It's a simple matter of cause and effect. Make one thing better and a dozen other things become worse."

"All they're asking you to do is deliver some letters," said Lenore.

"Impossible," said Aristo, sniffing with disdain. "After all, I'm not a common postman."

"I thought you were supposed to do anything we asked," said Nargis. "My wish is your command!"

"Oh, quite!" said the genie, giving her a withering glance that didn't have the desired effect.

"Well, if you're not going to help us, you might as well go back into your envelope," said Nargis, glancing across at Gil. "And we'll toss you in the wastebasket."

"I'm sure the spinster's hand would be happy to crumple you up and tear you to bits," said Gil.

The genie recoiled with alarm, turning to the two adults for help, but neither of them showed any sympathy.

"Hold on . . . Let's not be hasty, please," he said. "You've obviously misunderstood. I'll take your command under advisement, consider it carefully, consult my conscience and see if I can make an exception this time."

"What's there to think about?" said Nargis. "All we want you to do is take these three letters back in history to the people who were supposed to get them in the first place. After that, it's up to them to read the letters and do what they want."

"Let me consider it for a day or two," said Aristo. "Mull it over in my mind. You know . . . make sure it doesn't infringe on protocol."

"We don't have any time," said Gil. "Think carefully, because if you don't agree, we haven't got any reason to keep you around."

Aristo made a sour face. "Why can't you be like everyone else and ask for jewels, money or revenge?"

"Instead of making excuses," said Lenore, "I think you should listen to them and do what you're told."

"She's right, you know," said Prescott, who still wasn't reconciled to what was going on. "And there's nothing wrong with being a postman, by the way. It's a lot more honorable than being a genie."

"So, are you going to deliver the letters or not?" asked Nargis.

Aristo winced at the accusing tone in her voice. "First of all, let me explain that I have considered your request . . ."

"It's not a request," said Gil. "It's a command."

"Of course, of course," said the genie. "But you must understand that procedures have to be followed. We can't throw out a whole policy simply because of a sudden crisis."

"Listen," said Nargis. "I don't care what you think, or what policies you want to follow, we need to get these three letters delivered right away."

She held them out in front of her insistently.

Aristo frowned. "Unfortunately, I can't carry all three of them. As I explained to you earlier, we've had to cut back on services . . . retrenchment, cost cutting. We've reduced the number of wishes I can grant from three to two. For that reason, I shall deliver two of the letters but not the third."

Gil and Nargis stared at each other, then looked over at Prescott and Lenore.

"Two?" said Gil.

"Which ones?" asked Nargis.

"That's entirely up to you," said the genie. "I wouldn't want to make that choice myself."

"But why not three?" said Nargis. "That's not fair."

The genie had folded his arms and shook his head decisively. Even Nargis knew he meant what he said.

"It's beyond my powers," said Aristo.

"They're all important," said Gil.

"Yes, but . . ." Nargis hesitated. "If we can stop a war, that's the most urgent one of all."

"Sure . . . and the ransom note. Lawrence might be rescued instead of being killed," said Gil. "But what about Camellia Stubbs? If Ezekiel doesn't get the letter, he'll never know she loved him."

Lenore had moved across to where Prescott stood and now held his arm.

"If we have to leave one out, I guess it has to be the love letter," said Nargis. "Life and death are a lot more important than love."

The genie had averted his eyes, as if he wanted no part of this decision. Gil stared down at the carefully written script on the envelope, the flowing curves and arabesques of the spinster's hand. Just then, Nargis wrinkled her nose. The genie was already sniffing the air, and Gil wheeled around, hearing a knock at the windowpane.

In astonishment, they watched as five bony fingers pushed open the casement. A smell of lilacs and rotting flesh accompanied the disembodied hand as it hovered in front of them. Silently, the fingers moved toward the rolltop desk and settled on the piece of paper from which the genie had arisen. The knuckles cracked and the bones tapped softly, as if waiting for someone to make the next move. With a look of alarm, the genie had drawn back.

"I don't believe this...," Prescott muttered under his breath.

"You haven't got much choice," Lenore whispered as she squeezed his arm.

Nargis passed Aristo the letters one by one. First he took the coded message from Hermes. Then the scribbled ransom note. Aristo slid these into the pocket of his waistcoat. Camellia's letter remained in Nargis's hand. She held it out as the genie began to shake his head.

Snapping her fingers, the spinster's hand lifted the sheet of paper on which the genie's verses had been written. Very slowly and deliberately she began to crumple it up. The paper made a dry, rustling sound.

"Wait!" said the genie. Reluctantly, he took the third letter from Nargis and turned toward the hand. A crooked, skeletal finger beckoned the genie back onto the page. Without another word, Aristophanes Smith dissolved into ink dust and fell upon the crumpled paper. The hand then folded the poem along its original creases and stuffed it into the envelope, before carrying it through the open window.

Gil and Nargis had no time to react before it was gone. Along with Lenore and Prescott, they stepped across to the window and looked down at the yard, where dusk had settled. Below them on the lawn, they saw, or thought they saw, the figure of a postman walking across the grass and disappearing into the leafless trees.

41
Epitaph for an Unknown Postman

Trudging out of history, one slow stride at a time,
He shoulders a mailbag full of letters unreceived,
Lost missives, postcards gone astray, an errant rhyme.
Sore of foot, numb-kneed, the postman seems aggrieved.

One envelope he bears is folded neatly as a conscript's bed,
Each corner tucked and crisply sealed—chaste sheets
Bleached with fear—last words home, written at the dead
Hour of dawn, before marching into the killing streets.

He follows his own footsteps, ashen shadows upon the
   snow.
A nameless wanderer, whose story is a skein of yarns.
Unlike the anonymous soldier he has no tomb. Nothing I
   know
Will give him rest. No one stands at his crypt and mourns.

Then let these words be inscribed in stone; may fate dictate
On the postman's grave: "Better never than forever late."

Setting aside the poem, which he had just finished typing, Prescott glanced up at the photograph of Camellia Stubbs on his wall. For a moment his mind drifted back to the letter Nargis and Gil had found. Then his thoughts came to a sudden halt. The photograph looked different. It was still inside its oval frame but the image had changed. Instead of the silver-haired spinster in her black lace dress, the photograph was of a younger woman standing beside a writing table.

Reaching for his glasses, Prescott got up from his chair and squinted at the picture. The woman was definitely Camellia, but thirty years younger. She wore a long white gown, and her hair was open over her shoulders instead of being drawn back into a severe-looking bun. One of her hands rested on her hip in a carefree pose. Rather than the grim expression of resignation in the earlier portrait, her lips were parted in a bashful smile, as if someone behind the camera were teasing her. Camellia's other hand was placed on the table.

As Prescott examined the photograph carefully, he noticed something else that made him jump. On top of the table lay an inkstand. Even though it was a black-and-white photograph, he could see the glinting jewels and recognized the rich luster of gold. There was no mistaking it.

Turning quickly from the picture, Prescott rushed out of his office and up the stairs. He reached his study and shouted for Gil, who came out of his room just as Prescott was unlocking the lower drawer of his desk.

"What's wrong, Grandpa?" Gil asked.

"It's gone," said Prescott, holding the drawer open.

Gil looked baffled.

"The inkstand," his grandfather said. "I locked it in here for safekeeping."

"Do you think it's been stolen?" Gil asked.

"No," said Prescott under his breath.

"What happened?" said Gil.

"The genie has granted your third wish."

Still not sure what was going on, Gil's eyes traveled from his grandfather to the etching on the wall—the old picture from the *London Illustrated News*, of the siege of Ajeebgarh. But instead of a battle scene, the artist had drawn a peaceful picture of tea pickers with baskets on their backs. They looked as if they were walking through a maze of bushes that spread down the slope of the hill. In the background, Gil could see a placid river snaking out of the mountains, with the town along its banks, a cluster of rooftops, domes and minarets. The caption read

AJEEBGARH
Plucking the Finest Tea in the World

42
Erasing Fate

Sikander is dreaming. It isn't exactly a nightmare, though it isn't particularly pleasant either. He's on a battlefield with cannons firing, and smoke fills the air. Somehow, in the middle of all this, he finds himself fishing in a broad trench full of muddy water. He has cast his line into the middle, where a float made of peacock quills bobs up and down. As a cannonball screams overhead, the white bundle of feathers dips beneath the surface. He pulls back on his fishing rod and feels a tug at the other end. Moments later, three horsemen come galloping out of the smoke and he recognizes their tattered uniforms and broken teeth. One of them swings a sword at him as Sikander jumps aside. The three Tommies go riding off into the smoke. Sikander begins to reel in his line, but instead of a fish, he has snagged the blue bottle. The hook is embedded in the cork. Peering inside the bottle, he can see no message. Instead, a centipede crawls from of the mouth and onto his hand. Crying in panic, he drops the bottle . . .

Just then, Sikander wakes up. The sun has risen, glazing the windowpanes with a yellow sheen. He lies there for a moment, a cotton quilt pulled over his head. He is disturbed by the dream, not only because of the centipede, but because the day before, he'd gone down to the river, hunting for the bottle. Hoping to receive an answer from Gil, he had searched the muddy banks of the Magor, all the way from the railway bridge to the washermen's huts. Though he saw plenty of objects floating in the water, soldiers' boots and charred splinters of wood, there was no sign of the blue bottle. Despondent about his father's fate, Sikander had gone home. The bazaars were empty and his mother had made a gruel of barley flour, the only food she could find, but Sikander had no appetite and went to bed hungry that night.

Now, as he stares at the first light of dawn filtering through the windowpane, he realizes that something has changed. All of the windows in their house were shattered during the battle, but now they are intact. Slowly, he gets up from bed and peers through the glass. Instead of the blackened shells of neighbors' homes, the street has been restored. Sikander gasps with delight, wondering if the war was nothing but a terrible dream, something he will gradually forget. Yet he knows it happened. He has seen the death and destruction with his own eyes. He has heard the cannons and smelled the smoke. He has seen the post office in ruins and remembers his father being marched across the parade ground with the other prisoners of war.

At that moment he hears a soft shuffle of footsteps overhead.

Scrambling out of bed and through a curtained passageway that opens into the kitchen, Sikander races up the staircase leading to the roof. He takes two steps at a time and leaps onto the terrace. A whistle blows, and he sees a trail of smoke as the *Himalayan Mail* sets out on its weekly journey. He can see the mountains rising to the north and tea gardens spread across the lower slopes. In the other direction lies the palace, with its gleaming white dome and the pennants of Ajeebgarh rippling in the breeze.

As he rushes toward the pigeon coop, there is a flutter of wings, and a tall figure stands up, his beard brushed out from his cheeks. Mehboob Khan holds a handful of millet seeds with two white pigeons on his arm. Sikander runs across and throws his arms around his father, scaring off the birds and spilling the seeds. His father holds him tight, then lifts Sikander up, laughing with surprise.

"What's this?" he says. "Why are you awake so early?"

"I thought you were . . ." Sikander begins to speak but stops himself. "When did you get home?"

"Late last night," says Mehboob Khan. "You were asleep."

"But what about . . . the war?" Sikander asks. "The execution?"

His father raises his eyebrows and shakes his head.

"What war?" he says. "You must have been dreaming."

The two pigeons have returned and one of them settles on Sikander's shoulder. He can remember clearly seeing the white birds flying through the black clouds of smoke.

When his father sets him down, Sikander hurries back downstairs to get dressed. Then he heads out to collect lampblack from all of the houses in the neighborhood. At each door, when he knocks, he recalls the burning roofs and shattered walls. There is no sign of the battle now, and by the time Sikander has finished his rounds, he begins to question his own memory.

The calligrapher is waiting for him when he arrives, drinking his tea, as he always does each morning. Ghulam Rusool says nothing about the terms of surrender that he penned the day before. Instead, he gives Sikander instructions to make an ink for writing the verses of Ghalib, a poet whom the calligrapher admires more than any other. The old man asks Sikander to mix the lampblack with the burned wicks of seven candles. This is combined with two spoonfuls of rosewater and a drop of wild honey. When the mixture is complete, Ghulam Rusool dips his nib in the ink and begins to write in a flowing script. Sikander watches the characters stream across the page from right to left, recognizing the Urdu words. As the calligrapher dips his pen in the ink to begin the second couplet, there is a shout from the street. Sikander hears someone calling his name.

When he goes out to see who it is, Lawrence stands there in a white shirt and khaki shorts. Sikander is so surprised he cannot speak. As he glances at the calligrapher, he sees the old man wave, shooing him out of the shop.

Sikander grabs Lawrence by the hand and slaps him affectionately on the shoulder.

"What happened to you? How did you get back? I thought you were kidnapped!" he asks.

"I was," says Lawrence. "But my parents got the ransom note and they paid the money to the three Tommies, who set me free. Of course, the police caught up with them soon afterwards. Now they're in jail."

Sikander blinks in disbelief.

"I got your note," Lawrence says with a grin.

"Which one?" asks Sikander.

"The one you sent by pigeon," Lawrence reminds him, frowning. "Unfortunately, the Tommies ate the bird."

"I'm sorry I ran away," says Sikander.

"You didn't have any choice," says Lawrence. "By the way, what happened to your bottle and those messages?"

Sikander hesitates for a moment.

"Oh, that," he says. "It's gone."

As the two boys set off along the street toward the river, Lawrence describes his adventure with the Tommies, how they kept him hostage in the dak bungalow. He begins to tell Sikander how he escaped and was almost shot, then got lost in the forest and was bitten by a cobra . . . Suddenly, Lawrence stops and looks puzzled.

"Wait a minute," he says. "That couldn't have happened. I must have dreamed all that, but I'd swear . . ."

Sikander grins at his friend.

"Don't worry," he says. "The important thing is that you're safe."

Lawrence scratches his head. It seems as if everything has

changed, while at the same time nothing is any different than before.

✦   ✦   ✦

A few days later, they decide to go fishing again to Ambital, though this time Lawrence's father accompanies them. As they walk up the trail through the forest and look back on the town from the ridge above the tea estate, Lawrence seems to have forgotten about the threat of war. Sikander tries to tell him about the burning palace and the booming cannons, but Lawrence looks at him as if he's making it all up.

"Come on, it would never have come to that," he says. "The Russians backed down and the maharajah was allowed to keep his portrait on his postage stamps."

Sikander begins to argue but then thinks better of it. Instead he challenges Lawrence to a race, to see who will be the first to reach Ambital. Roderick Sleeman follows behind the boys, pausing to light his pipe.

When they reach the lake, Sikander and Lawrence stop for a moment to catch their breath beside the gravestone in the grass. Something is different, Sikander can tell, but before he is able to puzzle over the words, Lawrence is pulling impatiently at his sleeve. As he turns away, Sikander notices two names on the stone instead of one:

Sacred
to the memory of
EZEKIEL FINCH

MARCH 12, 1802—AUGUST 18, 1879

and his beloved wife

CAMELLIA

SEPTEMBER 3, 1812—AUGUST 19, 1879

Come live with mee, and bee my love,
And wee will some new pleasures prove
Of golden sands and christall brookes,
With silken lines, and silver hookes.

JOHN DONNE

43
Back to School

As the bell rang, Gil slid into his seat and arranged his notebook on the desk in front of him. It was strange to be back in school again; he felt nervous and excited at the same time. Some of the other students were staring at him, and he knew they were trying to figure out who he was and where he'd come from. Gil could hear whispers and the restless sound of homework papers being sorted. Somebody dropped a book and there was muffled laughter. The teacher was tacking sheets of paper to the bulletin board. When she turned around, the students settled down. Two kids came in late and hurried to their desks.

After all of the dead letters, the reluctant genie and the skeletal hand, it was nice to be back in an ordinary classroom again, where everything seemed perfectly normal and predictable. The homeroom teacher, Mrs. Ballantine, seemed nice enough. She introduced Gil to the rest of the class. He was relieved she didn't call him Gilbert. Nargis had made sure of that. Still, he felt uncomfortable as everyone's eyes turned on him, though soon enough they got down to work.

Convincing his parents to let him go to school in Carville had been easier than Gil had thought. His grandfather had done most of the persuading, telling them that he was happy to have Gil stay with him, and how it was better than putting him in a military academy.

"I think he's learned his lesson," Prescott told them over the phone. "And Gil seems to like being here. He's made friends. It would be difficult adjusting to a new place all over again."

His mother and father had come up and spent the weekend at the Yankee Mahal, instead of taking him off to Michigan. Gil had introduced them to Nargis and they had driven over to look at the school. Even though his father mentioned Howitzer Academy a couple of times, it seemed as if he too had decided it wasn't such a good idea after all.

"Michigan is pretty far away," his grandfather had said. "He'd have to fly home."

"I guess that's true," Gil's mother said. "Here you're only a couple of hours away."

"The two of us will drive down for weekends," Prescott said. "And you can come up any time you want."

Saturday night, Prescott introduced them to Lenore and they all went out for dinner together at a seafood restaurant. They had already agreed not to tell Gil's parents about the letters and everything else that had happened. It seemed as if everybody got along, especially Gil's mother and Lenore. He noticed that his father and Prescott even shared a laugh.

On Monday, there were papers at the school that Prescott had to fill out. Gil met the guidance counselor, who got his grades and other documents from McCauley Prep. By Tuesday morning, he was in class. Even after having been out of school for three weeks, Gil didn't feel he had fallen too far behind. In math there wasn't much of a problem because his teacher at McCauley had got ahead of himself and Gil had already done most of the work. In social studies they were doing a project on the Civil War and Gil joined a group that was writing a report on the Battle of Gettysburg. He and Nargis were in most of their classes together, except for PE and French, where they were on a different schedule because Nargis was taking Spanish.

When it was time for lunch, they met near the lockers and she took him to the cafeteria.

"You're lucky, it's pizza today," she said. "Not green Jell-O and tofu burgers."

Nargis led him to a table with some of her friends. She introduced him to a girl named Ming and a boy named Orion. They were talking about some horror movie Gil hadn't seen, but it didn't really matter. Orion kept imitating one of the ghouls who lived in a woodshed on a farm in the Ozarks. He made a creepy face and pretended to carry an ax in one hand. Ming and Nargis laughed. Gil didn't say very much, but he felt sure he was going to fit right in.

During the last period of the day, they had English and Mrs. Ballantine made them read two poems by Robert Frost, including one called "The Bearer of Evil Tidings," which was pretty good. Then she gave them their homework assignment. Each student was supposed to write a poem of their own and bring it to class the next day, to read aloud. Gil glanced nervously at Nargis, who was seated across the aisle from him. She rolled her eyes and grinned, as if to say, Don't worry, it's only homework . . .

44
Postscript

After school, Gil and Nargis headed home on their bicycles, but when they reached the cemetery they took a detour. Parking their bikes at the gate, they walked down the hill toward the chestnut tree.

"Maybe we should have brought another lobster trap," said Gil.

"I don't think so," said Nargis, wincing.

It was cold but clear, and they could see the harbor spread out below them, and the lighthouse in the distance.

The branches of the chestnut tree were bare, and dead leaves carpeted the ground. As Gil and Nargis reached the spot where Camellia's grave had been, they couldn't see a headstone. Together, they brushed away the fallen leaves, but there was no sign of the granite memorial, only brown grass and gnarled tree roots.

"It must be here," said Gil, circling the tree.

"Maybe not," Nargis said with a thoughtful frown. "If we really changed history, who knows what happened to Camellia? Maybe Ezekiel came back . . ."

"Or maybe she went to India," said Gil.

Just then, they felt a breeze and the dead leaves rustled at their feet. Both of them caught sight of a lone figure coming toward them up the hill. It was the postman in his gray uniform, stooped under the weight of his mailbag. He was almost the same color as the gravestones, and when he passed through the shadows of the trees he seemed to disappear briefly. Gil and Nargis could tell that he was coming in their direction. Both of them felt like running, but their feet were stuck to the ground.

"Yipes!" said Nargis under her breath.

"Stay calm," said Gil, even though his hands and knees were shaking.

The postman trudged up to the chestnut tree. With a tired sigh, he touched the brim of his cap in greeting.

Nargis tried to say "Hi," but her voice squeaked. Gil's mouth had gone dry and all he could do was nod. The postman reached under the flap of his mailbag. After hunting around for a moment, he took out a magazine in a brown paper wrapper. With a wistful wink and the faintest smile, he handed the piece of mail to Gil.

Seconds later, the postman was gone.

"What is it?" Nargis asked as she let out her breath.

"I don't know," said Gil, turning the magazine over in his

hands. On the other side, he saw an old stamp, and across one corner of the wrapper was written

Complimentary Copy

"Hey, it's addressed to you," said Nargis, pointing at the label. "Gil Mendelson-Finch. Open it."

"But, how could this . . . ?" Gil ran his finger under the wrapper and ripped it open. Inside was a copy of *The Atlantic Monthly*, but it was an issue from May 1, 1933.

"That's sixty years before I was born," he said as Nargis took the magazine from his hands and began to leaf through the pages. At first, there didn't seem to be anything interesting inside, but as she flipped back again, something caught her eye.

"Look! Here's a picture of the Yankee Mahal," Nargis said. It was a black-and-white photograph. In the foreground stood a man who looked as if he might be Indian. Nargis and Gil read the caption together.

The author, Sikander Khan, poses in front of Ezekiel
Finch's home near Hornswoggle Bay, Massachusetts.

"It can't be!" said Gil.

"Of course it's him," said Nargis, turning back a page to the title of the article.

RETRACING THE FOOTSTEPS
OF A YANKEE TRADER

At the beginning of the article was a short biographical note on the author.

MR. SIKANDER KHAN is one of India's most respected journalists. He is currently touring the world as a foreign correspondent for *The Statesman* newspaper in Calcutta. Mr. Khan recently visited Massachusetts. In this article, published here by special arrangement, he tells the story of Ezekiel Finch, a Yankee trader who made his fortune shipping tea from India to America. Finch's tea estates were in Ajeebgarh, which happens to be Mr. Khan's hometown, where he began his distinguished writing career as a calligrapher's apprentice.

Returning to the photograph, Gil and Nargis both squinted to try to make out Sikander's features.

Nargis started to laugh. "He's almost bald," she said.

"Of course. This magazine is from 1933," said Gil, pulling it out of her hands. "In this picture he'd be much older than when we were writing back and forth."

The Yankee Mahal didn't seem to have changed at all, with its heavy stone walls and slate roof. Standing in the front yard, Sikander had one arm raised. Gil and Nargis could tell he was waving at them.